Season of Infidelity

W9-CFW-781

VERTICAL.

Season of Infidelity:

BDSM TALES FROM THE CLASSIC MASTER

Oniroku Dan

Translated by Chris Violet

VERTICAL.

Copyright © 2010 by Oniroku Dan

All rights reserved.

Published by Vertical, Inc., New York.

Originally published in Japanese as *Bishonen* by Shinchosha, 1997.

ISBN 978-1-934287-36-1

Manufactured in the United States of America

First Edition

Vertical, Inc.
1185 Avenue of the Americas, 32nd Floor
New York, NY 10036
www.vertical-inc.com

Contents

Season of Infidelity

MY WIFE CHEATED ON ME twenty years ago. I was forty, she was thirty-four when she betrayed me. I can talk about it candidly now, but at the time I was a total mess. I look back at that period of my life and can say without exaggerating that I was on the brink of madness. I spent many restless nights, drifting in and out of sleep. While lying awake in the middle of the night I would plot out the murder of my wife and her consort. It wasn't like I neglected her sexual needs. We were as passionate in our relations as the contract of marriage obliged us to be, and so I would never have dreamed that she would feel the need to cheat on me. This is probably something you need to experience to understand, but there is nothing so miserable as a cuckolded husband.

The worst part of it was the fact that the man she was sleeping with was none other that my subordinate, my pupil, my trusted friend: Goro Kawada.

When I started my own production company, Oni Productions, in 1970, I hired Goro as a bondage supervisor. He was twenty-eight at the time. He was a bit of an eccentric, and was from the same Abeno district of Osaka that I'm from.

He worked with me on various S&M magazine shoots, bondage photography publications and pink films produced by Oni Productions.

Right after graduating from college Goro was hired by a major commercial company, but just two years in he had a fight with a superior and quit. Unemployed, he was reading the classifieds one day and came across a small ad I had placed looking for a bondage supervisor for Oni Productions. He worked freelance for us as what some would call a rope artist. Since we produced high-end photo books and films we needed a top-class rope artist to bind our models and actresses with intricate bondage quickly and efficiently. Anyone with a passion for tying women up is basically a little odd. So I was surprised when Goro showed up to the interview expressing a keen interest in S&M and bondage, since outwardly he seemed like an ordinary bookish type. He was fairly handsome, well-educated and had a knack for foreign languages. As a trial run I had him bind an actress for a pink film shoot. The actress had nothing but praise for his work. "If Mr. Kawada is doing the binding, I don't mind if it's a little tight," she said. If the models and actresses like the rope artist things go very smoothly.

I'd heard the girls complain on various occasions about other bondage guys. "I can't stand getting tied up by that idiot anymore. Get me out of this gig, please?" they'd complain, and I was getting fed up. "That one ties the ropes way too tightly," one would say, while another would complain, "He touches me in weird ways while he's tying me up," and so on. But once I started using Goro the complaints faded away.

"Mr. Kawada is so nice. He really pays attention to how we actresses are feeling while he's doing his work," they'd say. I think part of the reason he seemed so gentle was his slow, halting Osaka-accented speech and his slightly lumbering physicality that came off as endearing.

"Does that hurtcha? Be sure 'n tell me if it's hurtin', uh'kay? I'm doin' my best tah make sure it's nice 'n loose-like," he'd say, dragging out his speech while deftly wrapping the ropes around the girl's body, quickly finishing up the binding.

You'd never think from his slow, thick accent that he graduated from an elite school. He never once spoke like a member of the intelligentsia. There was something about his particular brand of openness, his unrefined nature and simplistic speech that touched something in the hearts of women he encountered. He was the type of man that I liked best, and I found him endlessly useful in both my personal and professional life. He helped me when I wrote my novels. He said he was a fan of my short stories when he applied for a job at Oni Productions, and would humbly point out mistakes in my stories and offer alternatives, proposing S&M scenarios that would be more exciting to the reader. For example, one time I was writing a period piece involving a punishment bondage scene which involved a rope wound around the torso and between the legs. "One rope won't be 'nuff when going between th' legs," he said, offering another idea. "If ya use two ropes, ya can spread open th' labia and expose her clitoris. Then ya can use a paintbrush 'r somethin' an' tickle 'n tease her right nice. The sweet humiliation'll overwhelm the woman's senses," he said. He would be very explicit and detailed in his ideas about bondage. What a dirty freak, I thought to myself, all the while taking careful note of his ideas. I ended up using most of his ideas in my writing. I couldn't deny that his influence made my writing all the more popular.

One of his main features was his expert ability to talk dirty. He was the life of the party and gave masterful lewd performances when the crew from Oni Productions would go out drinking after work. His sloppy western-Japanese accent and lazy enunciation helped take the edge off of the frank, blunt sex talk that would seem uncouth in anyone else. He wasn't yet thirty years old, but he had slept with a staggering number of women—college coeds, secretaries, other men's wives, etc. He'd brag that once he bedded a woman she'd be so blown away by his skill that she'd keep coming back for more. If he got really drunk he'd stand up, unzip his pants and show off his prized manhood. It was thick with a slight curve, and the head was large. He'd proudly tell everyone that when he was hard it would swell past seven inches. He was a bit of a fool, but he came off like a talented court jester so he didn't make anyone uncomfortable with his bizarre displays.

He'd drive women into an ecstatic, out-of-this world trance, bringing them to orgasm multiple times. His endlessly intriguing stories fueled my erotica novels.

I began to think of Goro as indispensable during the time I lived apart from my wife.

At that time my wife was a teacher at the middle school in S city, her hometown in Kanagawa Prefecture. I used to teach Japanese at the same school, and we soon fell in love. The principal acted as a matchmaker and we got married. She was the belle of the town, compared to that famous Komachi of the something or other. After we married I was on the receiving end of countless envious glares from other love-struck teachers at the school. My wife had graduated from an elite women's college in Tokyo, then spent two years studying in America. After returning to Japan she earned her teaching certificate and worked at her old middle school. I had tried to start up an underground theatre company in Tokyo but the whole project went belly up. I had to leave town to get away from creditors, and a friend got me a job at the middle school in S city working as a substitute Japanese teacher. I had mostly worked in burlesque and underground theatre, so my background and attitude towards teaching were totally different from my wife's. I only thought of teaching as a temp job, and planned to return to Tokyo and make a comeback. But then we fell in love, married, and her wealthy parents built a house for us on the shore. In order to repay their kindness I vowed to work hard as a middle school teacher and grow old and die in the countryside.

I can't deny that I enjoyed the life of a country teacher. The town was scenic and lovely, with the ocean close by. The air was crisp and clean, and the fish that we had for dinner was always fresh. To get to school from the house her parents helped to build we would ride along the coast overlooking the deep blue sea. The air would shimmer quietly in the heat from the sand dunes, and the fishing boats rocked gently at their anchors. The air smelled of salt spray and seaweed. It was an idyllic life, like a scene from a painting by an early Impressionist artist; I rode on a bike with my beautiful wife to school each day. I should have been perfectly happy, but after three years of idle countryside life my innate wanderlust began to stir. The first signs of trouble in our relationship started when I submitted an erotic short story to a shady publication in Tokyo. I craved a release from the monotony and washed-out feeling I had accumulated from working as a teacher in the countryside, but my choice of part-time employment offended my wife. Despite her foul mood, my story was popular with readers, and the publisher unexpectedly sent me a fat check for a manuscript and even called the teacher's office at the school asking me to write new stories for the magazine.

Before I worked as a teacher a novel I wrote was an official selection for a contest held by a well-known literary magazine. My wife was impressed with that novel—it was one of the reasons she was attracted to me—and so she was harshly critical of my "depraved" erotica.

"So if you like writing filth like that does it mean you're interested in that sort of deviant behavior?" she asked harshly.

I had done my best to hide my writing from my high-minded literary elitist wife. I couldn't write at home and couldn't write in the teacher's room at school, and with the deadline drawing near I had no choice but to make my students study by themselves so I could use the class time to write short stories. I even had the mailman hold any mail sent from the publisher at the post office, but one day while cleaning up my wife found a rough draft of a story I had shoved into the back of my desk.

"Oniroku Dan is your pen name, isn't it?" she hissed, making me cringe.

Somehow my wife had gotten her hands on a copy of *Mystery Club*, an S&M magazine, and tossed it in front of me.

Many years later I wrote an article about *Mystery Club*.

"*Mystery Club* was first published in the Kansai area of Japan in the late 1940s. Until this publication—so evil it would incur the gods' wrath—came about I had worried endlessly about my sadistic fantasies and had a bit of a psychological complex about my deviant sexual desires. So it was a real shock to me when I first saw this bizarre and wonderful publication with its images of nude women in bondage and stories of villains tormenting beautiful ladies. I felt like someone had seen right through my devilish fantasies and laid them bare on the page.

"I figured the editor of this publication must have been a devil himself."

I first made contact with that same editor when I was still working as a teacher in S city. I used the pen name Oniroku Dan and surreptitiously wrote *Flowers and Snakes*, a pulp smut novel. The *Mystery Club* magazine that my wife angrily thrust in my face was filled with images of women suspended from the rafters in ropes and tied up to posts, and the cover ran titles like "A Discussion on Female Bondage," "The Psychology of Sadistic Urges," "Can Married Couples Enjoy Bondage?" and on and on. And my bizarre erotic story was printed in the magazine. I thought my wife was getting worked up over nothing, but I could see tears in her eyes.

She was fixated on the fact that the stories were sexually perverted, but at the time I didn't realize that S&M was a specialty enjoyed by a certain segment of the population. I had figured it was simply a way to illustrate the power play that goes on during sex. Either the man or the woman takes control during love-making. When a man ties a woman up it awakens his latent desire to take a woman by force. I said it wasn't any different from any other kind of erotica, but my wife insisted it was disgusting, and pointed out the following passage to illustrate her point:

"Lady Shizuko lay bound in a spread-eagle on the bed. Her milky white thighs led up to her sex, covered in soft, warm, jet-black hair. Hot and dizzy with anticipation, she was wet with desire. Love juice flowed from her sweet ladyflower, and when the man pressed his member inside her, her organ responded like a shellfish, pulling him in with an impressive constricting force. Soon the contractions of her sex held him deep within her, refusing to let him get away, pulling him closer and closer. He felt her twitching with delight, the muscles of her sex constricting around his member. He trembled, barely able to resist the sweet sensation which reverberated through his very soul—"

This was from *Flowers and Snakes*. I thought it was a plain old sex scene, typical of the pulp erotic genre, but my wife knit up her brows and asked what I would do if people found out who the writer was. She imagined the police barging into our home and exposing me as the writer of this kind of filth. If the Japanese teacher of a local S city middle school was taken away in handcuffs for writing pulp porn it would be an embarrassment not only to the school but to the entire city, she said, letting her imagination run away from her. At the time my wife was the head of the English department at school, and at staff meetings I had seen her use this kind of tactic in arguments to wilt her opponents. Now she was using this same tactic to try and scare me. It's not that I hadn't thought about the possibility of being exposed. There had been exposés about contributors to erotic magazines and investigations and police searches of erotic production companies. I felt extremely guilty about writing dirty stories while my students quietly busied themselves with class work.

I had pictured local newspapers carrying the headline "Disgusting lecher 'teacher' exposed in porn raid," or something gruesome like that. It was enough to make me tremble with fear.

I ended up quitting my teaching job and leaving S city for Tokyo about a month later. A friend of mine had been bugging me for about a year to work in pink films or S&M publications. Since my secret erotica writing had been sniffed out by my wife, it was as good a time as any to take my friend up on his offer, but my wife was totally against it.

"So you're just going to go back to that ero-grotesque nonsense again, eh?" she asked bitingly.

I ended up going alone to Tokyo, but not without a prolonged battle of wills with my wife. That type of smart woman turns into a harpy when angry, and she didn't miss a chance to skewer any argument I could come up with and shower me with abuse and sarcasm.

"You really get off on that depraved trash, don't you," she'd say. "You can't resist the temptations of your old buddies' dirty offers. You're beyond help."

The more she nagged the more obvious it became that she was deeply jealous.

I figured I would try to make a go of it in Tokyo, but if things didn't work out after two years I'd return to S city, work as a public servant or something and live a quiet life with my wife. I told as much to my wife and her parents and finally I got permission to leave for Tokyo.

As soon as I started working in Tokyo things went laughably well. I hired aspiring actress Naomi Tani, fresh out of Kyushu, to star in the pink films I wrote. Riding on the success of those films I brokered a deal with Haga Publishing of Kanda to release bondage photo books, which were so successful I established Oni Productions and began publishing a magazine called *S&M King*. I had pocketed enough money to buy a house in Meguro almost exactly two years after I left the countryside. My wife had scorned my work as "ero-grotesque nonsense," but she had never dreamed I would be so successful in just two years in the porn business.

Around the time I was working on the *The Bondage Encyclopedia* with the photographer Kishin Shinoyama and the illustrator Akira Uno my wife left S city and showed up at my office to meet my coworkers.

"Are you actually interested in S&M?" she asked me. I answered that I was basically "normal."

The only reason I chose an abnormal niche to work in was that it was popular and therefore a lucrative part of the sex industry.

Once my wife saw that I was working with an internationally renowned photographer like Kishin Shinoyama her skepticism about my perverted work began to lessen. In the spring of the next year my wife quit her teaching position and moved to Tokyo. It was a chance for us to reestablish our married relationship. I had no objections to her living with me again. She was beautiful and intelligent and I always had great respect for her. I loved her very much.

Our separation of two years would end, and since I loved her I was satisfied with that, but there was just one small problem: I had taken a lover during our time apart.

I wrote earlier that I found Goro endlessly useful in both my personal and professional life, and this case was no exception. He was the one who acted as matchmaker and introduced me to my lover.

Before I bought my house in Meguro I had a small one-bedroom work-in apartment in Yoyogi. I needed a place other than the office in order to write my novels. One day Goro called me at my apartment.

"Hey boss, you must be lonely living apart from your wife for so long. I can introduce you to a girl you could have as your Tokyo wife if you want. It'd be under contract, of course," he said.

"Yeah, sure, introduce me to a nice girl," I said, half jokingly. Three days later Goro showed up at my apartment carrying a photo album.

"Do ya fancy inny of these girls?" he asked, opening the album. There were rows of pictures of college age girls.

"This section here is girls from K University, an'na this section is from C Women's College, an'na this part is T University," he explained, flipping through the pages. Goro's friend from college had organized a female student aid association. All the girls in the album were self-supporting students who were looking for a monthly sponsor to help make ends meet. Essentially these girls were being pimped by their male classmates. The girls all had financial problems, like their family had filed for bankruptcy or their fathers fell ill and couldn't pay tuition, etc. So they were looking for a gentleman who would pay for their tuition until graduation. Since the girls themselves had their own boyfriends the type of sponsor they were looking for had to be middle aged with a family. They didn't want to get involved with a young, hot-shot bachelor, no matter how rich he was. I nodded as I listened to Goro's explanation and flipped through the pages of the album. My eyes stopped on a photo with the name Kyoko Aizawa.

She had a slender, expressive face and medium length hair. I was intrigued by the sweet sensitivity I could see in her eyes.

"She's pretty cute," I said, pointing to her picture. Goro leaned over, saying "Section B number 4, righht?"

and pulled a notebook from the back of the album. She was a junior at Y Women's College and was majoring in British and American literature. She liked tennis and was good at playing piano, he explained, reading from the notebook. She was from Okayama Prefecture. Her parents ran a furniture store but the previous year they had gone bankrupt.

"Why don'cha meet her an'na see if ya like her? If she strikes yer fancy would ya be able to support her fer a year until she graduates?" Goro asked.

Goro set up a meeting between Kyoko and I a few days later at a café near Yoyogi Station. We agreed on a dating contract for one year.

I had an academic interest in S&M but had never actually performed any such act. I would indulge in fantasies about S&M while writing my stories, but after coming back down to reality I always felt too awkward and clumsy to actually try and tie up a woman. Oh well, I was a failure as an abusive lover. During any kind of confrontation I would always be the first to go to pieces.

I never used a rope or did anything S&M-like when I slept with Kyoko. I was perfectly satisfied with plain vanilla missionary position sex. I would have sadistic fantasies floating about in my head, and when we made love I would imagine all kinds of abuse I could shower on Kyoko, but in the end they were just fantasies I used to arouse myself. I was satisfied with that. Having normal sex while dreaming up abnormal fantasies was like masturbating while having sex. It was the same kind of intercourse I had with my wife. I'd imagine myself transforming into an ugly, hunchback janitor and taking my beautiful culture snob wife by force. I could thoroughly satisfy myself with that kind of fantasy while having typical monotonous sex. I could mentally blow off pressure from the inferiority complex I felt towards my wife with this type of masturbation/sex. I suppose her arrogant, groomed attitude and beauty aroused a sadistic tendency that I could fulfill through fantasy alone. Of course, neither my wife nor Kyoko suspected that I had entertained such twisted flights of fancy.

Comparing my wife and Kyoko, my wife had more of an intense, primal female urge that lurked deep within her. During sex, her passion would surge up and she would become unusually keen. The stereotype of a mousy librarian who goes wild in bed holds true with my wife. She would forgo all sense of feminine modesty or hesitation and become totally rabid with desire. She'd let herself go wild, begging "More, more!" and even though I enjoyed basking in extreme fantasies during sex I preferred the actual intercourse to be very simple. So when she'd go off the deep end I'd find myself growing hesitant and end up backing off instead of giving her what she wanted, but she never complained or showed dissatisfaction. Her intense sexual passion was momentary, but I felt guilty that I couldn't totally satisfy her. Whenever we quarreled she'd always talk me down. I have to admit she was endlessly fascinating to me.

Kyoko was very different from my wife, very docile, like a homemaker. She would show nothing but reserved feminine care and sensitivity towards me. I think those qualities were rare in college-age girls those days. My wife acted like my mistress and my mistress acted like my wife. Kyoko showed a womanly hesitation and bashfulness during lovemaking. She was slender with porcelain skin and a coquettish figure. Her legs were long and well proportioned, and the line from her knee to her foot was tantalizingly lovely. Her pubic hair was soft and light and curled like wisps of smoke. Her breasts seemed somehow not quite fully ripe, but they were perfectly shaped hemispheres with light pink nipples. I would cover her breasts, earlobes and neck with kisses, and that alone would cause her to writhe with pleasure and cry out in a soft, slightly sad voice. "Oh, no, I'm so embarrassed," she'd say, her voice trembling. When I reached a finger inside her sex she'd cry out "Oh! No! Please, stop!" furrowing up her eyebrows with embarrassment and trying to twist away. I loved the way she kept the game up and never let her feminine guise slip.

I was very satisfied with her. She'd protest verbally, her voice quivering, but her body told a different story. She was already soaking wet with hot desire. I'd climb on top of her and she'd spread her thighs wide open. I'd press my member deep inside of her sticky sweet sex and she'd be able to take in the whole thing. As I'd lose myself in the reverie of love-making—which was never anything more complicated than missionary style—she'd gasp, moan and cry out "Oh, I'm so happy," or "Please, daddy, don't leave me" as her muscles would begin to constrict around my member. I was very satisfied.

However, once my wife moved to Tokyo I had to be very careful to keep my affair with Kyoko a secret. My wife was a jealous type and a bit of a busy-body, so I had to go to great lengths to deceive her.

As soon as my wife was settled into our home in Meguro she had an announcement: "Next month Mack is starting an English cram school. I want to go and help him out twice a week."

Mack was an American, and worked part-time as a teacher at the middle school in S city. My wife and he would occasionally work together. He planned on renting out the second floor of a fisherman's hall to teach English after regular school hours and wanted my wife's help.

This Mack guy was ridiculously tall, and ever since we worked together at the same school I couldn't help but hate him a little. He would come to our house to discuss teaching plans with my wife, and since he lived alone she would feed him dinner before sending him off.

Eating with a foreigner is incredibly awkward. At first he'd try to make nice with me by making small talk in his poor, halting Japanese, but after a few glasses of wine he'd switch to speaking in English to my wife and the two of them would cackle like a couple of hens. I felt like they were going out of their way to exclude me from the conversation, and it made me very uncomfortable. It seemed like Mack was hitting on my wife right in front of me and getting away with it by speaking in English. It made me insanely jealous and after he'd leave I'd pick a fight with my wife. I honestly was uncomfortable with the idea of my wife working with Mack on his cram school, but she wasn't the type to be satisfied with just sitting at home all day doing nothing. If she was stuck at home all day she might get bored and start poking around and find out about my affair, so I decided reluctantly to let her go work with Mack just to keep her occupied.

Just one week after I agreed to let her go my worst fear was realized. I had gone to spend a night in Hakone with the staff of Nikkatsu to celebrate the opening of their Roman* Porno division. As we were hanging out in a hot spring spa I got a call from Goro.

"Boss, somethin' jus' terrible has happened," he said, sounding flustered. My wife had raided my apartment in Yoyogi.

My wife had wanted to go to my apartment and clean up for me, but I told her that the place wasn't appropriate for her. I would have bondage models and off-center S&M girls over to help me when writing, and told her it was best to avoid the area entirely. I told her the phone number for the apartment but didn't give her the address. I told her that I had put Goro in charge of cleaning and maintenance, so if she wanted anything she should just get in touch with him. I figured he was smart enough to parry any nosy inquiry she might have about the place. But my wife used the phone number to look up the address. As luck would have it, Kyoko was there when my wife found the place. Kyoko wanted to change the curtains and rearrange the furniture to her liking while I was away in Hakone.

"So this is how he's got it set up, huh?" she said, shocked at finding Kyoko, who had let herself into the apartment with her own key.

"Yer wife called me an'na told me to come to tha office.

* A common Japanese abbreviation for "Romantic" rather than the adjectival form of the city.

She scolded me, accusin' me of hidin' the fact that you hadda mistress. I wus so scared my knees knocked together. As soon 's she said 'You're th' one who introduced this Kyoko girl to my husband!' my mind went totally blank," Goro said. Hearing his play by play of what happened made me tremble so much I had to sit down.

Goro went to my office at once as my wife had ordered. Kyoko was shocked at the sudden intrusion, and my wife grilled her on why she was there. Kyoko could only think to say that Goro set up our arrangement and then high tailed it out of the office.

Goro sat politely on the floor as my wife reprimanded him for a long time.

"Yer wife is beautiful, but she's gawt herself a forked tongue. I wus totally defeated," he said.

His dull speech didn't convey the full extent of what she said, though I'm sure she gave him quite the verbal lashing. He then tried to make amends with her by taking her out to dinner. Once she began to calm down she talked about Shakespeare, he said.

"Shakespeare?" I asked, stunned. Apparently Goro had majored in English literature in college and told my wife that he studied Shakespeare. She latched onto the topic and launched into literary criticism of Shakespeare's works. Goro was so floored by my wife's erudite speech that he could only sit respectfully and listen in earnest to what she had to say. His docile modesty seemed to make a good impression on my wife.

Goro had succeeded in calming her down, but as soon as I returned from Hakone she unleashed her rage at me. I emphatically declared my love for my wife, and offered the painfully pathetic excuse that the only reason I had one of Goro's girls at my office was that I needed a model to work from in order to write my novels. "If you need a model so badly then maybe you're not good enough to be a writer in the first place!" she shot back. I couldn't get her to calm down. I was depressed about having to break things off with Kyoko when suddenly she declared:

"I'm going to borrow Mr. Kawada twice a week. I'm going to have him help me with the English cram school starting next month."

After each lesson they wanted someone to perform skits in English based on the topic of the lecture. She wanted to use Goro in those skits.

"His English is pretty good, so I think he'd be great for the skits. Plus, he has a car, so he can drive me to S city and back each time. And since it'll take some time until Mack's cram school is making money I'll have you pay for Mr. Kawada's time. That's your punishment for betraying me. Pretty fair, don't you think?" she said, jutting out her chin defiantly.

I called Goro to see how he had answered my wife's request. "I wus afraid she'd cook up somethin' worse if I refused, so I agreed ta do it," he said. He had been overpowered by my wife.

"Then I have a favor to ask of you as well," I said. "Mack has the hots for my wife. I want you to act as her bodyguard and make sure he keeps his hands off of her." Her discovery of Kyoko and coercion of Goro was beginning to work out in my favor, I thought. The next month Goro started driving my wife to and from S city twice a week. I wasn't thrilled by the fact that my wife had snatched away my best assistant, but she would say, "Mr. Kawada really puts his heart into the work. It's a great help." She seemed very thankful so I couldn't stay pissed off at her for long. "His English is so good you can't hear a trace of his thick Osaka accent that he has when speaking Japanese. Weird, huh?" she laughed.

Three months passed. I started to notice that my wife seemed more refined, more sensuous. Her beauty seemed somehow reinvigorated. Perhaps it was a result of her pride in her work, but she suddenly seemed more polished, dressed more sharply and went to the beauty parlor more often than when we lived in S city. She bought fancy clothes. She brimmed with a rich beauty. When I looked at her I felt a sudden ache, but whenever I tried to reach for her she flatly rejected my sexual advances. "You're on probation for six months, pal," she said.

She was still punishing me for having a mistress in Tokyo.

I got depressed. A doubt began to creep in: what if my wife, suddenly so recharged in her femininity, was now cheating on me? Even so, I never dreamed that her lover would be Goro.

I asked a friend of mine in the porn industry if he thought I had reason to be suspicious of my wife's beautiful transformation. He answered that husbands have two strong conflicting emotions on the subject of their wife's fidelity. On the one hand men want their wives to take a lover, but on the other hand men are terrified of being cuckolded. If one's wife catches onto to that hidden conflict she may very well choose to have an affair.

I was especially worried since my wife had extra reason to cheat, given the fact that she discovered my affair with Kyoko. She might sleep with someone else out of revenge. But I had imagined that Mack was the prime candidate for a lover. I had asked Goro to keep a watchful eye on their interactions. Basically, I wanted him to act as her bodyguard. To think that the one I chose to keep my wife faithful would end up being the one my wife was unfaithful with!

I found out about their affair in the most ridiculous way. One night Mack called, drunkenly slurring his speech. "Your wife and Misser Kawaada seem to have somethin' going on," he said surreptitiously.

I was shocked to get a tattle-tale call from Mack of all people, since I had suspected him of trying to sleep with my wife. I tried to ask him a question but he just rambled on in drunken English before saying "Good Night," and hanging up. I immediately rang my house in Meguro. It was one of the days that my wife went to work at Mack's cram school, but she should have been back long before I called at one o'clock in the morning. She wasn't there. I kept calling until she finally picked up—at two a.m.

She said there was an accident on the highway and the traffic was so bad it took forever to get home.

"Mack called and said there's something going on between you and Goro," I announced.

"What?" she yelped wildly, then collected herself a bit and said, "That's really not funny," then laughed. She explained that the three of them had gone out drinking after class and Goro and Mack had gotten into a silly quarrel. Mack probably felt slighted and decided to get revenge by calling me up and telling me a baseless rumor, she said.

I just couldn't bring myself to believe that Goro and my wife were sneaking around behind my back.

I figured Mack must have just been drunk and let his imagination run away from him. However, the next day Goro stopped by my office unexpectedly and laid out the truth right then and there.

"Last night yer wife called me 'n told me that Mack had told you 'bout us. I panicked. She told me that she denied everythin' an' ordered me ta do the same if I knew what was good fer me."

I had to force myself to calm down. I went to the fridge and grabbed three beers and put them on the desk.

"Mack followed us in his car. He saw us go into tha hotel. I thought 'n thought about what to do but realized there was jus' no way t' hide it."

My hand trembled as I opened a can of beer and poured it into a glass.

Apparently the first time they slept together was the third time he drove my wife home from S city. They stopped at a love hotel called Meguro Emperor near the Meguro train station. It was all I could do to keep from having a blubbering, messy fit. I feigned calmness and offered Goro a beer. If that was their first night together then they had been having an affair for over three months.

"Well, what's done is done. I'm actually kinda glad

that you're being honest with me," I mumbled.

"I feel jus' awful about havin' deceived you, tha one person I owe so much to," he rambled on. What the hell are you talking about, I thought, doing my best to keep my roiling anger from bubbling over. But I just couldn't believe that my rational intelligent wife would fall prey so quickly to this lady-killer. When I asked for details on how their affair started Goro answered, "Mack was'a gamin' for yer wife. It pissed me off. If she slept with Mack I figgered it would be a total loss so I stepped in an' offered myself instead, thinking that was 'least a li'l better." It was odd to hear him explain that he thought it would be better to sleep with my wife than to let Mack have at her. He seemed very out of sorts, and drained his glass in one gulp. Goro tried to seduce her during the drive home. At first she was hesitant, but eventually she gave in, saying, "Can you promise me you won't tell a living soul for the rest of your life?" giving him a penetrating look. After that they went to the hotel. "Was the sex any good?" I asked, feeling desperate.

"Yessir, she got me off three times," he said bluntly, and I nearly spit out my beer. *She got me off three times.* His boastful remark rang in my ears for quite some time.

I felt like I was trapped in a nightmare. All I could think of was the times Goro would get drunk and show off his huge dick to anyone who would look. I felt a burning jealousy welling up and drilling through my heart, thinking about how many times he used that fat skewer to spit-roast my wife. I could practically hear her cries of pleasure filling the night.

I felt a kind of masochistic need to hear what exactly had happened between them. I asked him to give me the details, knowing full well that this kind of topic was his forte.

"I'm really not comfortable wit' talkin' 'bout your wife that way, sir," he said with a nervous laugh and tried to change the subject, but I scolded him into submission. I felt like I was able to exact a kind of revenge on my wife by hearing every detail about her disgraceful behavior under Goro's sexual ministrations. I kept refilling his glass with beer, and eventually he felt bold enough to talk about what happened. As he spoke he seemed more and more despondent, but I was desperate to know.

I was used to hearing him talk about his sexual conquests, but none of those stories made me feel as hot and bothered as when he talked about his affair with my wife, her crazed, wild, foolish sexual actions. I felt jealousy boiling up, and got a raging hard-on to boot. Hearing this man talk about how he made my wife squirm and writhe in pleasure was a huge turn-on. I'm disgusting, I thought to myself.

"I'm sure you weren't satisfied with just plain vanilla sex, were you," I asked, my face twitching into a lopsided smile.

"Actually, yer wife is quite a masochist, sir," he replied, much to my surprise. "Intelligent, well-bred women like her'll put up a front 'cause they're proud, but eventually they let go and end up enjoyin' the man's sadistic advances," he explained. "I'd only started to gently break 'er in, so I didn't do anythin' more than bind her arms. But that was enough to git her to have multiple orgasms." I was so shocked to hear this that my mouth fell open. I'm sure I looked half insane. He listed off the following points about my wife. Each thing he said shook me to my core.

1. Your wife is an expert in fellatio.
2. Your wife has a fantastic vagina.
3. She's an extremely eager student in bed.

Whenever I asked my wife to give me head she was apathetic about it. She would do it out of a sense of marital obligation, but only half-heartedly. She normally gave up after only a minute or so. But with Goro she would flick her tongue back and forth along the back of his penis, lift up and suck his testicles with her mouth; she showed the finesse of a pro, he said. I asked if he was the one to teach her those tricks, but he said she had plenty of natural ability. As a sadistic act he would tie her up naked and make her sit on the floor in front of him and then force his hard dick into her mouth. She apparently had the kind of personality that could be easily trained into enjoying that kind of "slave play."

"That's how we usually start our sex play. That's how I got off first." Basically she let him come in her mouth. After hearing that I suddenly felt dizzy, like I was floating above my chair and my head was a helium balloon about to drift away. Seeing me turn pale made Goro ask if he should stop talking about the affair, but I told him to go on. I must have looked like I was on the verge of tears.

Once he was nearing the point of no return he would ask, "Ma'am, I'm gonna come. Is that okay?" almost unable to hold back. She would then take his member out of her mouth for a moment, her eyes wet with effort and emotion and tell him, "Yes, please give it to me. I'll prove my love by swallowing all of it."

Then she'd wrap her lips around the head of his penis and vigorously bob her head up and down. The friction between his penis and her mouth would make little spurting sounds. "It felt so good I couldn' take innymore. Once I came in her mouth she'd moan and suck it aawll back. It was absolutely mind-blowing."

I felt the blood drain from my face. I got up, walked in a circle once around my chair then plopped back down. Just hearing that she swallowed made me feel like I was about to faint. It was appalling.

"You said she has a great vagina. What do you mean?" I asked, trying desperately to appear calm. I tried to keep him relaxed by forcing a lewd grin.

"Yeah, she's got an amazin' snatch. You never noticed? She's great to fuck."

She's great to fuck, I repeated silently to myself. Seeing my dumbfounded expression made him smile an obscene lopsided smile.

He explained that he would make her lie on her back with her arms bound, then tie her ankles together so her thighs were spread open butterfly style. He would then place a pillow under her hips so her sex was totally exposed.

Basically he would force her into a humiliating position for foreplay. He then went about exploring her sex bit by bit. This is where the conversation turned to allow Goro to show off his vast knowledge of female anatomy.

He took a pen and a piece of scrap paper from my desk and quickly started sketching a picture of my wife's genitalia. He skillfully drew the slit of her exposed vagina and the aroused, protruding clitoris. As he explained each part of her sex I had to continually use the back of my hand to wipe away the sweat that began to pour off of my face.

I had never examined my wife's private parts with such exacting detail. He explained that he would gently spread her labia with his fingertips and draw his tongue along the length of her lady flower. Then he would suck her clitoris, drawing it up and out, which would cause her vaginal muscles to contract like a clam. He dove into his favorite topic of conversation, his drawling western accent making him seem all the more lively. One of his specialties at this point in the foreplay was to make her say aloud the embarrassing words used for the female genitals.

"I'd tell 'er 'I don't want to hear nuthin' about no Shakespeare. Tell me what this is called," he'd say. She'd gasp as he touched each part and as she cried out the name of each part her clit and the lips of her vagina would swell up, engorged with arousal.

"Hot love juices woulda flow out of her as if some inner dam had broke," he told me with a far away look on his face. Those fluids were her body's response to the semen she had swallowed earlier, so he dutifully lapped them up. After all that intense foreplay your wife could come many times, he said. "She's be so turned on, I'd slip jus' two fingers inside of her and her milk white thighs woulda twitch with pleasure. Her rumpled hair woulda sway back and forth an' the muscles in her neck would stretch with excitement. Her cries of pleasure always seemed a li'l fancy-like. I liked that," he said.

Three months later, my wife and I decided to get a divorce. In those three months I felt I had aged three years. I almost never went home to our house in Meguro. I would shut myself into my apartment in Yoyogi all day long. Sometimes I'd wander like a vagrant through the streets of Shinjuku, bar-hopping through the ramshackle pubs of the Golden Street area. After I drank myself into a stupor I'd stumble back to my unmade bed and pass out. I didn't bathe for days on end and my fingernails grew long and collected grime.

The floor of the office became sticky with dirty residue but I didn't have the energy to worry about cleaning up. I cancelled almost all the jobs I had lined up during that time.

I kept a cassette player near the head of my disheveled bed. I made a habit of listening to the tape in the player before falling asleep.

It was a recording of Goro and my wife. On the night he confessed the affair, I coerced him into secretly taping one of their lovemaking sessions. Goro had recorded many of his conquests by hiding a recorder under the pillow or below the bed. He had a nasty habit of playing the tape back during one of his drinking parties when he wanted to elaborate on the stories of his exploits.

"Please, anythin' but that!" he said, trying to wriggle away, but I absolutely insisted. No matter how many detailed stories he told me of my wife's greedy passion, her crazed disgraceful actions in bed, I just couldn't believe it without some kind of evidence.

He says he forced her to talk dirty and name aloud the parts of her sex, but I just couldn't believe that my wife of all people would lose herself so completely to someone like Goro.

I finally was able to force him into getting me a taped recording of one of their lovemaking sessions.

A few days later he showed up at my office. "It went really well," he said and played the tape for me. I realized then that he hadn't been exaggerating about my wife's wild behavior.

At first I heard Goro trying to coerce my wife into it, but she put up a coquettish resistance, her voice shy with hesitation. But after a few minutes of enduring Goro's foreplay her voice changed and she moaned and cried out.

"Ah, please, please fuck me!" she practically howled.

It was indeed my wife's voice, but I had never heard her cry out with such terrific, forceful passion before. The cries were so sexual, so vulgar that it was as if my wife was possessed by another woman's voice.

Just as Goro had said she had many, many orgasms.

When he would bind my wife's arms behind her back he would either have her straddle him face on while he was sitting, or have her facing away and straddle him. When in these positions she would spread her thighs wide and sit on his legs. This way his penis could penetrate her fully, he explained as we listened to the tape.

"There're several merits a' these straddle positions,"

he said, sounding like a sex expert. "The man can use his hands free-like, to rub her tits, suck her nipples, 'r slide a finger down and stimulate her clit. 'Cause her arms're tied up she can't hold onto th' man. This agitates her, so she pumps her hips as hard as possible. So she ends up gettin so excited she gets off verra quick. Also, 'cause he's sitting down the man won't get worn out in this position. He can take his taahme and control how fast he gets off."

Just as he said, my wife seemed to be having the time of her life.

"*Oh, Mr. Kawada, I'm—I'm coming. I'm coming again. Please, come with me. I want you to come—*"

Her erotic cries continued for a bit until suddenly she screamed out, "*Yes, YES!!*"

"*Oh, you bad boy. How many times are you going to get me off?*" she moaned, sounding slightly vexed. After a moment she started crying out again with such rapture, it was as if she was melting to the core with sheer joy.

According to Goro, he then had her straddle him while facing away so her back was pressed against his chest. He was penetrating her from below and behind. "This trick is really only possible if tha man has a big e-nuff dick," he bragged.

"I was rubbin' her breasts which were shoved up by the rope 's I banged her. It's really useful ta have a mirror when doin' this position. I had us facin' the mirror in the love hotel dead on so she coulda see everythin'."

Apparently the sight of her own sex-intoxicated expression, misty eyes and bound body made her unconsciously move faster and harder against his body. She looked absolutely fascinated as she stared transfixed at her own reflection. "She was so amazed by her own sexiness she couldna speak. I'd then watch her and time it so we came jus' at the same time," Goro explained. Indeed, I could hear both of them groaning at once as they climaxed together.

Every once in a while as they were screwing in this position my wife would suddenly cry out, "No! Anything but that!" in an angry, startled voice.

When I asked what was happening, Goro said he would tease her by taking his penis out of her vagina and pressing it up against her anus. "Won'cha let me fuck ya here?" he'd whisper, his breath tickling her ear. She would frantically struggle and pull away. "There's no way you could fit that huge thing in there," came her voice on the recording. After hearing his explanation it made sense why she was saying that. His huge member would rip her delicate, tight anus to pieces, I thought.

"That's th' only thing I haven't been able ta do with her. It'll take some time 'til I'm able to talk her inta anal sex," he said as I listened keenly to the tape.

Three months later, I was sitting alone in my apartment nursing a severe hangover.

I couldn't bear to even think about all the problems that had come about over the preceding few months because of my own mistakes. I was sick and tired and hated everything, I thought, pitying myself. I shut out the world and locked myself into my little apartment. "I should never have brought my wife to Tokyo. I should have just left her in the countryside," I thought, bitter with regret. But it was too late. I thought back longingly to the simple days when my wife and I would ride our bicycles to school along the winding coast, the brilliant scenery and the sea salted air just a memory away. I missed the perfect, clear sky and the deep azure sea.

I pictured my wife in a white blouse and black skirt, her hair fluttering in the sea breeze as she rode along the coastal road, looking so fresh and healthy. I could hardly believe that ten years of such bliss were destroyed completely in less than a second.

Our friends thought it was ridiculous of us to suddenly get divorced just because she cheated, but after sleeping with Goro of all people she had discovered the deepest secrets and highest ecstasy of fantastic sex. There was no way for us to go back to the way we were. What's done is done, I moaned to myself.

Listening to the recording of their lovemaking became my only joy in my solitude. I'd suddenly find myself aroused and end up masturbating to the sounds of their intercourse. I felt that masturbating like this was disgusting, but I spurned myself on, thinking I had no reason to pretend to be pure and innocent anymore.

I was aroused by the fury that burned within me in the face of hard evidence that my wife had in fact cheated on me, and also by the belated realization that my wife was exactly the type of woman that I had always longed for. I never noticed the intense sexual passion that lurked deep within her. Goro was the one who sensed it and drew it out to its fullest extent. It took someone like Goro, so full of life and energy with his ingenuity and clever techniques to coax the masochistic nature out of my wife. Not a moment went by without hearing his boast: *She got me off three times.*

He told me they usually had marathon sex sessions lasting three or four hours. I feel foolish to even think of comparing myself to him, but when I slept with my wife we got off only once, and the whole ordeal took twenty minutes, tops. Knowing now how insatiable she was with Goro, I'm sure she was never satisfied with me.

And yet I still found it so hard to believe that sexual dissatisfaction would lead a woman like my wife to fall for the dubious charms of a vulgar lady-killer like him.

Anyhow, there was no denying the fact that my wife was transformed by her affair with Goro. She was now totally out of my league, and of course her previously tender emotions for me began to cool and she turned away. I ached at the sight of her newly rediscovered beauty, but there was no way we could stay together. We divorced and she moved back to her parent's house in S city.

On the day as she planned to leave Tokyo she stopped by my Yoyogi office. Unusually, she was wearing a fine purple gray Oshima kimono made of soft, unbleached silk bound with a silvery obi. She had brought a bouquet of flowers which she unwrapped and arranged in a vase on my desk. She had stopped by to present me with flowers as a farewell gift.

"Mr. Kawada and I decided to break up a week ago," she said, sitting properly before me. I could see the pale porcelain skin of the nape of her neck under her kimono. She looked so young, charming and vivacious. I felt the dull ache of lingering affection as I gazed at the graceful, perfect oval of her face.

"Why break up with him now? So what if I know about it. You and I are strangers. We've divorced," I said, somewhat sarcastically.

"No, that kind of relationship was never meant to last," she said, sighing and turning her face to the wall.

I had received a thank-you note and a letter of resignation from Goro a few days earlier. After seeing me locked up in my office exhausted from worrying day and night he had finally realized the extent of the damage he had done and felt incredibly guilty. *I've done you a great disservice and I'm ashamed of myself,* etc., etc., he apologized. He also wrote that he planned to break things off with my wife.

He may have felt sorry for me after seeing how depressed I was, but I was pretty cruel to him as well.

Once I knew of their affair, I used the apparent shock to turn the tables on him and spurred him on to play a trick on my wife.

I made him record one of their nights together, capturing her lovely, sensuous cries on tape. When I made him play the tape for me I laughed like a madman. He probably thought I had completely lost my mind, degenerating into a totally perverted smut writer. I was drunk off of the feeling of sheer revenge, retribution for all the contempt, disdain and scorn I had weathered over the years. At the same time, I was utterly heartbroken and totally exhausted. I barely registered the fact that Goro had turned in his resignation.

"Let's drink a farewell toast, with brandy," my wife said, pulling a bottle from the sideboard. She handed me a glass, then bowed her head, saying, "Thank you for taking care of me for such a long time."

"I'm going to meet Mr. Kawada at the Yoyogi train station, then he's going to drive me back to S city. It'll be the last time I see him," she said. Goro had said that he wanted to see my wife in a kimono just once, which was why she was dressed up tonight.

Seeing her looking so fascinatingly lovely in a kimono made my heart ache. I felt like I was seeing her beauty for the first time. She had gone to a salon to have her hair set in a full shape that curved away from her face. She looked like a perfectly innocent young wife. I couldn't help but feel incredibly jealous that she had gone to such lengths preparing herself for Goro.

I refilled my brandy glass and drained it in one swallow.

"So, are you gonna go to some cheap hotel and fuck him?" I asked, using the guise of drunkenness to curse at her. My wife gave a faint, bittersweet smile and refilled her own brandy glass.

"No, of course not. We've totally cut things off and promised to just remain friends. We'll probably go out to dinner tonight though."

"What the hell are you talking about? He's a skirt chaser. As soon as he lays eyes on you in your cute little kimono he'll get all horny and beg you to let him fuck you," I said, getting angry.

My wife, however, refused to cave under my angry

tirade. She was either drunk or just plain defiant when she said, "And so what if I do? I'm not married to you anymore, remember? It's none of your business!"

Her breath smelled of liquor, and as she spoke a faint gleam of ruthlessness flickered in her eyes. It made her seem all the more sexy. It irritated the hell out of me.

"You of all people..." I said, my voice rasping in my throat.

"I can't believe you would fall for a bondage freak like Goro, of all people," I groaned. "He's a playboy, a pervert. He's a degenerate who boasts about you and what you're like in bed to anyone who'll listen," I cried, blurting out the worst things I could think of Goro. The more I spoke ill of him the worse I felt, feeling self-loathing and self-hatred welling up and pushing me to the verge of tears. My wife, however, stood up for him, and it was like pouring gasoline on a fire.

"Mr. Kawada is nice, and he's cute, and he's sincere," she said. I was shocked at her irrational, schoolgirlish defense of him. She insisted that she didn't just sleep with him out of her sexual frustration in our marriage. She found him simple, fresh and charming. Maybe it was some inner motherly love or instinct that drew her to his juvenile delinquent behavior and attitude. "He would brag about how once he slept with a woman or tied her up she would be totally under his power. I don't know, he touched something in me that desired real pleasure," she said. "And once I knew just how amazing he was in bed I should have resented him for his arrogance, but instead I got more and more caught up in my feelings for him. I found myself longing for the next time we could go to the love hotel. He showed the outer limits of sexual pleasure. He even found my G-spot."

He was the first one to teach me what a real orgasm was, she rambled on, leaning on the crutch of alcohol to brave through the blunt conversation.

"You said you hated bondage. But then you go and get tied up by Goro."

"Yeah, I did. And I liked it. It all depends on the man who's doing the tying," she said, letting a leering grin creep into her face. "Being bound spread-eagle on the bed and having my private parts examined was so embarrassing I could hardly stand it. But he was so skilled with his tongue he got me so hot I didn't care what he did, it all felt so good. He's the type of guy who can stay very cool and watch calmly as I twitch and writhe, my body burning with desire from the tips of my toenails to the top of my head. I'd get so worked up I had no idea what I did or said."

"Yeah, and I heard you'd totally lose control and flail around begging him to fuck you as hard as he could," I said, trying my best to be nasty.

"Ah, he told you that?" she said, without any hint of discomfort. "That bad boy," she laughed to herself. "Yeah, I might have said something like that. Who knows? I don't even remember what I was thinking. I just followed his orders."

"You even let him come in your mouth. You swallowed his semen," I said, digging in further.

My wife suddenly turned defiant. "Yeah, I did. It didn't matter whether he came in my mouth or my pussy. I was just focused on getting him off because I was in love with him. He drove me crazy so I wanted to return the favor. You don't really think about consequences when you're in the moment like that. When he was drunk sometimes it would take half an hour to get him to come with a blow job. My jaw would be numb with pain the next day," she said, practically gossiping. I felt like she had whacked me over the head with a club. Just some time ago I had been spun like a top by Goro and his indecent talk, and now my wife was tearing me to pieces with her side of the story. I felt totally defeated. I'd thought I was so smart to get revenge with a secret recording of her having sex with Goro. I thought I could pull her off of her high horse with that, but now I felt utterly inferior and knew I had lost the game.

Having finished up the last chores of our divorce my wife got ready to leave. I felt an overwhelming sense of bitter jealousy clawing its way through me. My wife took one look at my face, which was twisted with anger, and said, "I should probably leave before we get into a fight."

I was drunk. I poured myself another brandy and hurled abuse at my ex-wife. "You're a whore. You're a lewd, loose woman. Just the type that asshole Goro likes," I spat at her, letting my inferiority complex creep in.

"That perverted freak is aiming for your asshole. You're not really against it, are ya. Why not let him do you up the ass," I yelled, feeling desperation choke me. She turned and looked out the window.

"You're right," she sneered. "Mr. Kawada told me all about the pleasures of anal sex. If he's so intent on having it that way I just might grin and bear it. Since I'm a newly minted divorcée I have no anxiety or resistance to hold me back. So I just might find out what it's really like tonight. Should be fun," she said, tossing the words out like so many bits of pulp fiction dialogue. She opened the door and walked out.

After she left I drank myself into a blind rage, writhing and storming about the office. After a while I crawled into bed and fiddled with the cassette player. I listened to her satisfied cries of pleasure, thinking to myself she's probably crying out even more awfully than this right now, having anal sex for the first time in her life. I imagined her in bed with Goro and started to jerk off. I turned my bloodshot eyes to the drawing Goro had made of my wife's genitalia. I gazed at the picture, transfixed. I could almost hear Goro explaining every detail to me.

I love the shape of yer wife's pubic hair. It's not too thick, not too thin—a perfect oval shape of soft, lush hair. First, I'll use tha tip of my nose t' nuzzle through the thicket of her hair.

As I'm a' doing this she'll open her thighs wide, tremblin' slightly and letting out the softest moan. At that point I'll push my fingers inside of her 'n spread her open. She'll already be soakin' wet, the lips of her vagina swollen and open, and her clit engorged 'n standin' tall—

I kissed the picture he had drawn of my wife's genitalia. And I wept. Hot tears of regret rolled down my face, bitterness far beyond the simple emotions of lingering affection or embarrassment running down my cheeks. I wept.

Pretty Boy

EARLIER THIS YEAR, I HAD a reunion with an old schoolmate, Mikio Yamada, at the rustic Shuzenji hot springs. It had been forty years since we had last seen one another. I had received a letter from Mikio's daughter who lived in Tokyo, saying, "My father is leaving Osaka for a quick vacation. Would you be so kind as to spend some time with him? He has cancer, and I'm afraid he won't make it through the summer." I think his daughter felt the need to fulfill the obligations of filial piety in the last months of her father's life. Apparently Mikio had told her that he wanted to see me one more time.

My second grandchild was born recently. There's an old saying that when your second grandchild is born two of your friends will die. However, two of my friends had already died the year before. Hearing that Mikio was dying made it seem like the gods were overdoing it a bit. I suddenly felt old and lonely, and realized that I had entered the sad winter of my own life. I went out to meet Mikio at his hotel at the Shuzenji hot springs on the appointed day.

Mikio was staying at the small and quiet Inabaso hot

springs inn. A river quietly burbled past the inn, and a grove of bamboo out back gave the place a rustic, country feel. The innkeeper led me to a tatami-floored room. From the window I could see farmland that had been left fallow for the season. In a small, dark pond next to the veranda black carp swam in the cold water, as reflections of cold white clouds drifted across. Once in a while a distant train whistle would echo sadly through the countryside.

Soon after I arrived Mikio Yamada made his way to the room, helped along by his daughter and her husband. I was shocked to see how much he had changed in forty years. His once corpulent figure had withered and wasted away, his bony, tall frame topped with pure white hair. His face was gaunt and pale. He looked like a ghost.

"Hey buddy, how're ya doin'? Been forty long years, eh? Damn long time, 'a dare say," he said. Until I heard his peculiar western-Japanese accent I could hardly believe this was the same Mikio I knew all those years ago. He was so changed by age, so thin and wrinkled that I could hardly recognize him at all.

He was wearing the lounge robe provided by the inn. He took slow, halting steps, entered the room and sat in front of the table. He introduced his daughter and son-in-law, who lingered in the corner. His daughter was petite with a round face, and the shape of her eyes reminded me of Mikio in his youth. Her husband was an architectural engineer in his mid-thirties, with a head full of thick black hair.

They were both very hospitable and well-mannered. "Thank you so much for coming all this way," his daughter

said, bowing to me. After the waitress brought in dinner
she offered beer and sake all around. Mikio barely touched
the food or drink, however. He ordered plain water and
took the array of colorful little round pills that his daughter
laid out on the table before him.

"I've heard so much about you from my father," she
said, offering me sake. "You were the leader of the jazz
band in college, right?"

"Yeah, the band at K University was top notch. Ev'ry
one said they were real professional-like," Mikio interjected,
happily nodding along to our conversation. His body was
thin and wasted, but his mind was still sharp. He was still
able to talk up a storm, but occasionally he'd run out of
breath or suddenly have a coughing fit.

He told his daughter and her husband all about how he
was actively involved with the bands at K University and
worked on the live music festivals there. He remembered
it all as clearly as if it had happened yesterday. That's right,
that's how it was, I thought to myself, suddenly nostalgic
for those days.

"Were you actually in the band, father?" the son-in-
law asked.

"Nah, I was the head of the fan club though. I loved
jazz, and wanted t' hang out with tha cool-kid musicians.
Right, buddy?" he said, looking to me for confirmation.

"Yeah, we were real lucky to have yer father lookin'
after us," I said, slipping into a western accent after hearing
Mikio speak. "He was like the patron of our band, y'see," I
said, and his daughter and her husband seemed impressed
by that.

"Is that so?" she asked, refilling my sake cup.

"Hey, tell 'em about the good ol' days, will ya?" Mikio said, his face crumpling into wrinkles as he recalled the details. "The someone-or-other kingpin of the south, and the something-or-other," he said, talking about the old gangs of Osaka. Mikio was on good terms with the neighborhood yakuza at the time, and he was a peculiar presence at school. I was sure there were countless stories of his fights around town, but I couldn't remember any of them. I did, however, remember his mysterious girlfriend, Mariko. She was registered as a social studies major, but she worked as a nude model for a sleazy magazine and rumors that she was a prostitute were rampant. She was a troublemaker. We called her "The Bitch" and "Slutty Mary." Once she started dating Mikio we called her "Miss Yakuza." Everyone thought they were the strangest couple.

I wasn't really sure if it was appropriate to discuss his old lewd flings in front of his daughter, but he didn't seem to have a problem with it. "That Mariko, she died 'few years back. Cancer, jus' like me," he said, suddenly mentioning her name. I was surprised to hear that she had died.

"Your old flame Kumiko also died. Everyone's jus' droppin' like flies, they are. Next it's my turn I guess y'could say."

"Father, please don't talk like that," his daughter chided, repulsed by the morbid talk.

"Alright, alright," he said, giving her a smile. "But this guy here," he said, pointing a finger at me, "he messed aroun' with another beauty while he was with Kumiko, y'know. Already gettin' in trouble wit' love triangles in college. Quite the man, right, buddy?"

I would never have thought that he would bring up my bizarre love triangle from way back when. There was a time when thinking about that mess made me want to scratch my face off, I was so totally ashamed of what I had done. But that was forty long years ago. Mikio and I were both sixty-five years old. Most of my memories of those days were faded and fuzzy, but I could remember that rape incident as clear as day.

It all started when I was in my junior year at K University. I was having problems with two members of the fair sex. It was pretty intense to be a college kid dealing with something as intense as a love triangle. Mikio said I messed around with a "beauty," and I just suggested I had problems with two women, but one of them was in fact a man, a homosexual. The words "transvestite" or "queer" stir up images of someone that's a professional pervert, but I didn't sense any such nuances back then. To me, he was simply a pretty boy.

His real name was Kikuo Kazama, but as the son of the distinguished Wakamatsu family renowned in the world of traditional Japanese *buyou* dance, he took the stage name Akika Wakamatsu. Since middle school he had performed in theatres alongside famous founders of buyou dance schools.

He entered an honors program at the K Academy, then moved up to an English major at the university proper. I met him when he was eighteen.

As soon as he set foot in the university he joined the

traditional Japanese music club. Or rather, he was abducted into the club by upperclassmen who had been lying in wait for the famous Kikuo Kazama to enroll in their school.

The Japanese music club met in a room on the second floor of the central auditorium, right next to where my jazz band practiced.

Since our practice rooms were right next door we had to compromise on when to hold rehearsals. Our band was a twelve-piece swing band, and when we crammed into the room and started jamming the walls would literally shake. The force of our playing would blow away the *shamisen* and little *shakuhachi* flutes playing in the room next door.

One day Kikuo Kazama stopped by our rehearsal room.

"Excuse me, but we would like to rehearse from three o'clock 'til four o'clock. Would that be alright?" he asked, hoping to negotiate. There was a music festival sponsored by the culture club coming up at the Asahi Music Hall, and we were rehearsing at a frenzied pitch. Our swing band was the main event at the music festival, the audience at standing-room-only status, with the girls screaming and shouting. "Encore, encore!" they'd all cry after our set. The traditional Japanese group was dull in comparison, and unpopular among the young college crowd, so they were like mice coming to negotiate with lions. Normally, I'd tell them to go pound sand. "Y'all can rehearse when we're done," I'd tell them bluntly. But as soon as I saw Kikuo's face, the angry words died in my throat.

As I looked at his beautiful features something stirred within me, and my heart began to ache. His clear, jet black eyes, his elegant nose, the flower petal shape of his lips—

He had an ethereal beauty. It was the first time in my life that I had ever looked at a member of the same sex and felt my heart skip a beat.

But I wasn't the type to fall for boys. I wasn't supposed to be queer.

If this kid was a woman I'd follow her to the ends of the earth, I thought briefly.

"M'kay, fine, y'all can rehearse first, then. But after an hour, we'll start bangin' and jammin' and tearin' away without holdin' back, 'right?" I said, with only a mild threat in my voice. I'm sure the only reason I agreed to let them rehearse was the strange, throbbing ache induced by seeing Kikuo's beauty.

"Thank you so much!" he said, his eyes gleaming with happiness at my concession. He bobbed his head in thanks.

I realized that he was the son of a famous line of *buyou* dancers shortly afterwards. Aside from his beauty, he spoke properly, with elegance. He had the noble, supple grace of a kabuki actor who played female roles. I'm sure all this was the result of years of training as the son of a distinguished artistic family. I wasn't at all interested in buyou dance, traditional Japanese music or even kabuki, so I really had no idea how famous Kikuo was among talented young buyou dancers. I did, however, notice that whenever the Japanese music club started rehearsing, girls would fill the corridor and squeeze in to get a look through the window of the practice room.

"That's Akika Wakamatsu!" "He's so beautiful!"

Until Kikuo joined the club none of these trend-followers ever paid any attention to the Japanese music group.

On the day of the music festival the audience responded to the traditional Japanese music like never before. I'm sure it had a lot to do with Kikuo's presence. A group of geishas from Sonezaki-shinchi were in attendance—something one would never see at a typical college music festival. I was hoping that the conductor would announce that Kikuo would be dancing to a piece played on the shamisen, but Kikuo entered wearing long black formal robes and wide legged *hakata* style pants, and sat before a *koto* harp set against a folding screen painted with gold leaf. Another "old boy" of the Japanese music group with a long beard appeared with a bamboo flute. They began to play Michio Miyagi's pioneering *koto* composition, "Springtime Sea."

Kikuo's fingers dexterously plucked out the melancholic melody, the notes fluttering out like so many cherry blossom petals. As a fellow musician I could tell that he had complete mastery over the instrument. The sounds of the harp and the flute floated out through the hall like the first springtime thaw melting the snows and flowing down the hillside. The audience sat and listened, entranced.

After the song ended the music hall reverberated with applause. Just before the curtain fell, Kikuo removed the harp pick from his finger and quietly bowed his head. It was simple, clean and beautiful.

Soon after the music festival, Kikuo Kazama and I found ourselves involved in a special relationship, but even now I can't really remember how it came about.

It might have been the long, fawning letter I sent after seeing his performance at the festival. Now that I think about it that letter was like a love letter. "I was very moved by your magnificent performance. I couldn't help but gaze at the serenely beautiful profile of your face as you lost yourself in the music. I was overwhelmed with a strange, powerful sadness at the knowledge that such a beautiful and talented man existed." My face flushes red just thinking about the conceit I put down on paper.

"I wanted to thank you for the letter you sent."

As I was eating lunch in the cafeteria Kikuo suddenly spoke to me from behind. My heart leapt into my mouth at the sound of his voice. I didn't understand why I was experiencing schoolgirl crush-like symptoms whenever Kikuo was around. He was carrying a lunch tray and asked, "May I join you?"

"Yeah, sure, go ahead," I said and made room for him at the table. My body felt like it would burst into flames of joy at the prospect of sharing a meal with Kikuo.

I would steal an occasional upward glance and my heart would dance anew at the sight of his elegant, sensuous features.

His features were of the same sort I fantasized about my ideal woman—intelligent, refined, graceful, beautiful.

However I couldn't say that I was in love with a man.

I had noticed that boys in high school and college would take out their pent-up sexual energy with each other, but I had a girlfriend, Kumiko Iijima, who helped me out with my sexual frustrations. I never felt the need to experiment with boys.

Kumiko was in the same social studies major as Mikio's girl, Mariko. She was also the lone female member of the swing band. She played guitar. She was one of the guys, and very cheerful and lively. But if Kikuo was a woman I had to say that he would be far more beautiful and, well, feminine. It was more than just his physical beauty. His bearing, speech, intelligence, elegance and refinement made Kikuo more feminine than Kumiko, more feminine than any woman I had ever known.

"I plan on keeping that letter in a special place," he said. Once in a while he would shyly turn a coquettish gaze to me.

I suddenly remembered how one of the guys in the swing band said, "He's a fag, you know."

He might have been a homosexual, but I didn't care.

He only played the *koto* harp as a hobby, but his skill so overwhelmed me and I was deeply moved by his performance. I was in awe. If that qualifies as homosexual love, then I guess I had a platonic gay crush on Kikuo Kazama.

I told him that I never really cared for traditional music, but after hearing his wonderful performance I had to give him a rave review. It made me look at traditional music in a whole new way.

"Well, traditional Japanese music is secluded, feminine music. The jazz and swing music that you played is very open, very masculine. When I heard your swing band my heart danced," he replied. Even though he was born in Osaka he spoke with a standard Japanese accent. He said it was because he was used to formality, but as he got to know someone he would relax and use a soft western accent. I'm sure the formal speech was a result of his strict upbringing.

As we got closer, he started speaking with an accent. He also started sending letters to my dorm.

Last night, you were in my dream. You were on a stage, playing the trombone.

You were wearing a white tuxedo pinned with a red rose. You looked dashing. I think you were playing "Moonlight Serenade." All of a sudden the curtain flew away and the stage disappeared, and you were surrounded by glittering stars—

This kind of girlish fantasy was further evidence that he was gay. I could tell that he was beginning to have feelings for me. While it was true that he got me all flustered, I would never have believed that I would end up the object of his affections.

We would meet by the entrance to the Nishinomiya train station near school and from there ride the Hankyu rail to Umeda, where we would take the subway to Nanba. We often went on boys-only dates like that.

He asked—or rather, he ordered me—to go with him to see kabuki theatre. I had a hard time with kabuki, but he would say "I really wanna see *Umeyuki in the Fall!*" or "You have to go with me to see Danjuro's *Sukeroku!*" I couldn't say no. He made me pay attention and learn all about kabuki during those days.

We saw *Sukeroku: Flower of Edo.* The set was the interior of the Miuraya brothel, designed with red-latticed wood. The luxurious and gorgeous staging was something

I had never experienced. As a kid who only played horn in a swing band on dinky little stages, I was totally blown away.

Including the outer robe, the costume for Agemaki, the top courtesan at Miura, had five layers. Add the obi belt and the tall geta sandals, and the entire get-up weighs over sixty-five pounds.

"I once wore a courtesan costume like that for a parade scene in a festival. It's so heavy that I had to really work hard just to walk. But my father scolded me, saying if I used too much masculine strength it ruins the image of a female character." Kikuo laughed softly and reached out and placed his hand over mine.

Sitting there in the dark of the theatre, the touch of his hand was far more exciting to me than any explanation of the kabuki play on stage.

So I found myself being pulled into a homosexual relationship and began to feel baffled by these new thoughts and emotions. I was worried whether I was really queer. I bought *Psychopathy of Sex* by Richard Freiherr von Krafft-Ebing in a used bookstore.

The all-female Takarazuka Troupe's Grand Theatre was right near the K University I attended, and the area was dotted with the homes of star performers. The famous beauty Yachiyo Kasugano who played male roles in the company also lived near the university. I would often see her surrounded by a group of fangirls whenever she left the house. Her fans acted like ladies-in-waiting serving an androgynous mistress. These followers worshipped Yachiyo like an idol, and there was no mistake that those girls harbored homosexual feelings towards her. Yachiyo, the object of their sapphic affection, was beautiful, talented and indeed androgynous. I realized that her fans' feelings were similar to the feelings I had for Kikuo.

After a performance at the East-West Kabuki Festival, we headed out to Dotonbori, to a small restaurant called Taruhei on a street near the Hozenji temple. Kikuo wasn't much of a drinker, but that night our table was invaded and he was cornered into drinking sake.

The intruders were geisha from the Souemon district.

"Ah, Mister Akika Wakamatsu is here!" said one, spotting us in our small tatami room, and a group of three geishas and their clients all cried out in glee upon seeing Kikuo.

"Would y'mind so terribly, if we were to join ya there?" asked one of the geishas. They probably figured it wouldn't be an intrusion, since we seemed like just two regular college kids having a drink. The three geishas and their richly kimono-clad customers squeezed into our small tatami-mat room.

One of the geishas asked what dance Kikuo would be performing in the fall festival sponsored by X Daily, and another asked him if school was getting in the way of his dance rehearsals. They kept ordering decanters of sake and serving Kikuo.

"I take dance classes during the day, but ah jus' don' seem ta get any better. Ah'd love to hear secrets 'bout dance from a performer such as yourself," said the eldest geisha, refilling Kikuo's sake cup.

Kikuo's lips curved up into a faint smile. "There was

a geisha once whose tabi socks were loose and wrinkled. That's a disqualification for geisha dancers," he said, and all the geishas quickly checked their own socks to see if they were wrinkled.

"I think the hardest part of Japanese dance is getting the right tabi. A dancer moves across the stage lightly on the tips of the toes, or springs quickly off the heel. The tabi needs to fit tightly even as the dancer twists and turns their ankles. A dancer's tabi are like a boxer's gloves. We often order special tabi and then spend time breaking them in. The best tabi have a deep cleft, which make the feet look small. Also, they have to be tightly fitted so absolutely no wrinkles show. I think beautiful feet are the number one important thing for a dancer," Kikuo said. As he spoke the geishas and their clients who had been sitting before a casually dressed Kikuo suddenly straightened up and listened respectfully. I was getting bored, however.

One of the gentlemen guests addressed one of the geisha. "It's a bit sudden, but since this is a great chance, why don'cha have Mister Akika listen t'one of yer songs, there." The geisha he spoke to was petite, with finely drawn eyebrows. "I've been practicing folk songs. Would ya be so kind as to listen to one?" she asked, and Kikuo, beginning to show the effects of all the sake, nodded his consent.

The petite geisha went out to the front where she had left her shamisen. She untied the cover, saying "Alright, I'll sing 'Black Hair' for ya."

She started to pluck out the tune on the shamisen, but Kikuo, who had been drunkenly nodding off, suddenly called out for her to stop. "Play that last part one more time," he said.

The geisha was totally taken off guard. When she finally finished the song, Kikuo asked for the shamisen. "The tuning's a little off," he said, and laid the instrument on his lap and twisted the tuning pegs to adjust the pitch. Kikuo's body swayed slightly as he closed his eyes and began singing "Black Hair" and everyone gave a small cheer.

When I let down my long black hair at night
On the pillow that we shared—
When I sleep alone
That same pillow is my enemy.

I only knew jazz music, so I didn't care for the song, nor could I tell when it was played well or poorly. It was my first time hearing Kikuo play and sing like that. I thought he was very good at balancing the shamisen with the singing. I got up to use the restroom, and as the song ended I could hear the geisha burst into applause.

"I've jus' learned so much! I get it now! So that's how ya find the pick-up note."

"Th' song's so lovely, an' your intonation is amazin'. I was shiverin' with pleasure."

I heard the geishas cooing their approval as I stepped out of the restroom and headed to the wash basin. Kikuo was there, holding a hand towel.

"I'm so sorry. I thought 'might be fun t' have some geishas join us, but now I feel like I'm the one bein' made to act like a geisha," he said, apologizing. I was flustered. He must have thought that I got up and left the room because of the brazen behavior of the geishas.

"Let's go home soon, m'kay?" I said, handing him back the hand towel. Kikuo bashfully turned his tipsy, slightly bloodshot eyes to me and said, "Let me stay at your place tonight."

"What?!" I barked, surprised.

"It's a pain to go all the way back to Ikeda at this hour. Plus, if I go home drunk my father will yell at me," he pleaded.

It was just a twenty-minute ride on the Hankyu Takarazuka line to the Ikeda station from Umeda, but Kikuo's house was another fifteen-minute walk from the station through Mt. Satsuki Park. "I'm too scared to walk alone in the dark all the way home," he whined.

"Alright, fine, but I'm warnin' ya it's a rickety li'l place, an' it's so cluttered ya can barely walk through. It's not the type a' place a li'l rich kid like yourself would feel comfortable in."

"Don't be mean. Please? Can I stay over?"

I nodded, and he smiled brightly and ran out to the reception area to phone home. I often let my bandmates crash at my dorm if they were too drunk to get home, and I welcomed that kind of thing. But with Kikuo, it was as if a female friend had suddenly asked to spend the night, and suddenly a strange tightness came into my chest. I found my thoughts racing ahead, wondering if something might happen between us. I had no idea what went on between two men in bed, so I didn't know quite what to expect. But seeing how things were shaping up, I knew that something was bound to happen.

My dorm was near the Umeda train station on the Hankyu railway in the Juso district. It was on the second floor of a building behind a street lined with shops. The first floor of the building housed a store selling Buddhist altar supplies. The entrance to the dorm was in the back, though, so we never disturbed the elderly woman who ran the shop.

I had been to Kikuo's house once.

The drive from the gate to the house was lined with gravel, and the pathway had large, round stepping stones. There was a blackened bamboo open verandah and a simple, large stone bath outside. You could see the cliffs jutting off the mountains from the garden, where exquisitely shaped black pines stretched out their branches. I watched Kikuo take over the day's lesson from his father and teach a class of young female dancers dressed in yukata in the large Japanese style rehearsal hall. The son of the distinguished family who lived in that so-called Palace of Ikeda was coming over to stay at my dirty little place, where the sliding doors and floors were covered in a faint film of dust.

"Surprised? Whaddya think, as dirty as I said it was?" I asked, and he said, "Yeah, I guess it's true what they say: maggots grow in homes run by men," cringing and laughing. He refused to listen to my protests when he started washing the dirty dishes left in the sink. "You're makin' me feel guilty," I said as he picked up the stuff I had left scattered all over the floor. This guy is totally a woman, I thought to myself while feigning ignorance as I watched him work.

I had an extra futon stored for guests, and Kikuo helped me pull out the futons from the closet and spread them out on the tatami floor. We crawled under the covers and talked for a long time. Kikuo told me that he knew he was gay from a very young age—when he was seven, eight years old. Apparently it was customary for young boys of buyou dance households to wear girls' kimono until they entered kindergarten. When he first had to give up wearing those pretty kimono upon starting school he remembered feeling very sad. Since puberty, he noticed that he preferred boys, and his first love was a kabuki actor, but because of the huge difference in their ages his love remained unrequited. He felt absolutely no attraction to women, and even when he looked at nudie magazines he wasn't aroused at all.

When he was seventeen he was taken by force by his step-uncle. He hated the guy, and was so filled with disgust over what had happened that he wanted to die. I persisted in asking him how a man takes another man, since that was what I was most curious about.

"No, that's really not something I can put words to," he said, a little peevishly, but he reached out and held my hand under the blankets. Suddenly he jumped up from his futon and came over and snuggled his body against mine. I felt like a woman had just leapt into my bed, and I was very aroused.

"I'd like to take you just like your uncle did," I said, my voice trembling.

"No, not that," he said. "Just hold me. That's enough."

His words said one thing while his body said another;

he started writhing and pressing his body tantalizingly against mine. I held him like I always held Kumiko, wrapping my left arm around his back and placing my hand on the base of his neck, holding him close. I pressed my cheek against his. Kikuo let his body go slack in my embrace, and he began to pant excitedly. He eventually pulled away, placing both his hands on my neck and covering my cheeks and throat with impatient kisses.

"I love you, oh, I love you," he gasped, and suddenly planted a kiss squarely on my lips. At last, I thought, Kikuo and I are bound with this kiss. My heart beat faster.

I had very little sexual experience, so I was totally done in by Kikuo and his ingenious kissing skills. I felt dizzy as he darted his tongue in and out, licking and caressing my mouth. He then wrapped his tongue around mine, and then pulled my tongue into his mouth with a quick sucking motion. His rich kisses shook me to the core and I found myself utterly entranced.

Kikuo got up and turned off the bright overhead light and switched on a dim lamp on the nightstand. His feminine face was lit with bewitching sensuality. Already, I thought of Kikuo as a beautiful, fascinating woman, not just a pretty boy. I urgently went about trying to take off his underwear. Once he was completely naked I kissed his cream-colored skin desperately. Without thinking, I slid my hand between his thighs, but he stopped me, and turned a sad face to me. He covered his loins with his hands and said, "That's the one part I don't want you to see. I'm a boy, I'm sure it would just disappoint you. I don't want you to end up hating me."

But I was persistent, and kept trying to pry his hands away from my goal. Finally he said, "Alright, but you have to get naked too," and sat up to help me remove my shorts.

And then I learned what happens when two boys have sex. When I think about it now, it seems embarrassingly silly, trifling. And since it was my first time it was almost like we were just playing doctor.

We pressed our bodies close together, kissing lustily, and started rubbing off each other's dicks.

Kikuo's penis was totally normal. It was of average size, the head was properly cleft, and the foreskin was drawn back as it should have been. His dark chestnut colored pubic air curled delicately around the base, and like any other boy's, his penis swelled and stood erect as he grew aroused. This was my first time doing anything like jerking off another guy, so I didn't really understand the technique and I was so flustered that I'm sure I was very terrible at it. Even so, Kikuo acted more feminine than most women, writhing in pleasure at my touch. His upper body rocked as he thrust his hips, crying out in a high-strung whisper, "Oh, I'm so embarrassed. Please don't leave me after seeing me like this."

Without thinking, I ended up climbing on top of Kikuo. This would be normal when having sex with a woman—missionary style—but with Kikuo, I couldn't finish us off in this position.

But I only realized this dilemma after I was bearing down on him, and couldn't help getting all flustered. The sound of our engorged penises rubbing together filled me with an unbearable frustration. And then Kikuo did something odd. He guided my penis in between his thighs, then closed his legs tight, allowing my member to slide against his clamped inner thighs. Basically, he was trying to get me off using his thighs instead of his hands. He began thrusting his pelvis upward against mine. He moaned, "Come, baby, I want you to come," in a whining, pleading, begging whisper as he undulated his hips. He turned his sensuous, gleaming eyes to me, and I thought how feminine, how sexy he was. I gazed into his sad, expressive eyes and felt a shiver run down my spine. I kissed him again and again, but for some reason I wasn't able to climax just from the friction of his thighs.

I got tired and pulled away from him, sitting on the disheveled bedding. Kikuo sat up, saying, "I'm so sorry," and pressed his cheek sadly into my chest.

"Don'cha worry about it. Ya don' need ta worry 'bout me so much. It's fine," I said. Just knowing that he really wanted to get me off made me happy. I placed my hand on his back and tried to comfort him. Again, Kikuo did something odd. He turned over onto his stomach on top of the blankets.

He covered his face with his hands and turned his back to me. He started shaking his finely muscled buttocks back and forth. It seemed like he was inviting me to do something, and the way he moved his hips was definitely erotic, but I didn't know what he wanted me to do. I just sat there staring, slack jawed, at this display, thinking, "What on earth is this kid doing?"

A few days later I got in touch with an upperclassman, Ken Togo, who knew a great deal about gay sex. I told him that Kikuo had tried getting me off by placing my penis between his thighs. Ken explained that that was called "intercrural sex," a kind of sex that homosexuals indulge in. He also explained that when Kikuo started waving his arse around it was an invitation to have anal sex with him. When I heard that gays are divided into "tops" and "bottoms," which refers to their anal sex position, I let out a surprised yelp.

"What kinda fool are ya? How can ya be messin' around with a queer and not know how we have sex? Moron!" Ken said, laughing.

I protested, saying there was no way an erect penis could fit into such a small hole. Ken just laughed, and called me a moron again.

Apparently they use lubricant so it goes in smoothly. Plus, the anus can expand to take in a penis. "I'm sure he was totally ready for you," he said. After graduation, Ken Togo formed a gay rights alliance and was active in politics. During college he was an enfant terrible who had an affair with a bank manager, so I'm sure his interpretation was correct.

I'm sure it made sense to a gay man to have sex like that, but at the time, I had a hard time believing that something that seemed as wrong as anal sex between men existed in this world.

If Kikuo had explained such a practice to me that first night I'm sure I would have been shocked, but I might have gone ahead and tried it anyways. I think he was too embarrassed to explain such a method out loud. He looked so miserable, waving his buns back and forth. "What's the matter whitcha?" I asked, laughing, and gave the moving target a smack. He suddenly stopped moving. He probably thought I was such an ignorant boor.

"Let's get some sleep," I said, feeling exhaustion creep up. I pulled him close and tried to get him to go to sleep, but he slid his hands down to my loins and grabbed hold of my cock.

"How can ya sleep with a ragin' hard on like this?" he whispered into my ear, and started to creep his way down my body. I suddenly felt the sensation of his tongue on my member, and gave a shout of surprise. I had never received oral sex before.

Kikuo stuck out his tongue as far as it would reach and began flicking it back and forth along the length of my enlarged member. He flattened his tongue and licked up my penis, then rested my testes on his tongue and sucked them up. It felt amazing, and I wanted to wallow in the intense pleasure of it, but embarrassment took the lead and I yelled for him to stop what he was doing. I tried to push him away from my crotch.

I felt humiliated to have a man down there sucking my penis, and I tried to writhe away from his grasp. But Kikuo turned defiant. "No, I'm determined to get you to come for me," he said, holding me down fiercely. His tongue techniques made me swell even bigger, and soon he placed the whole thing in his mouth and started bobbing his head vigorously up and down, sucking. Whatever, I don't care anymore, I thought desperately and let my guard down and allowed myself to enjoy his ministrations. Between his skillful handiwork and the intense sensation of his mouth

I was soon overwhelmed with a sizzling feeling of pleasure, and I came a few minutes later. When I climaxed he held me in his mouth, and waited until my orgasm subsided. Afterwards, he went about cleaning me up, gently licking my member clean.

I never even dreamed that I would find such pleasure at the hands of another man. I was in a daze, stretched out like a well-fed cat on the futon, but as the glow began to fade a feeling of disgust began to slowly well up. Thinking that another man had made me climax suddenly gave me the sense that I had been somehow tarnished.

Finally, Kikuo raised his head. His face was flushed with effort, and as his face drew near to me I could see excitement and arousal in his gleaming eyes. "You came for me! I'm so happy," he said and stood up, still naked, and went to the kitchen. He got a towel and soaked it in warm water from a thermos, wrung it out, and brought it over. He then carefully cleaned up my wilting penis.

He showed a woman's sensitivity, apologizing profusely for doing such a "mean thing" to me as he gently cleaned me up. He's so sweetly feminine, I thought to myself. It was like he had transformed into a harlot in the heat of the moment, seducing me and insisting that he bring me to orgasm, and as soon as it was over he became gentle and innocent, apologizing for his unladylike behavior. "I'm sorry," he said, gently kissing my thigh. It was this display of generalized feminine sweetness that made me feel better about the whole situation.

"I feel like I've done somethin' bad to Kumiko," he suddenly said. He knew that I had a girlfriend.

"Oh, no. I feel like I've gotten involved with a married man," he added. As soon as I heard Kumiko's name I got angry. I couldn't help but compare her to Kikuo. He was far more sensual and giving than she was. I had slept with Kumiko countless times. We would always end up in boring old missionary position, with me thrusting away monotonously. There was hardly ever an emotional exchange. She was never embarrassed by sex, and was too vain to put up a show of feminine hesitation or restraint. I couldn't complain too much, since the sex served the purpose of relieving a fair amount of tension. However, she would often orgasm first, and after that she found it annoying to have me pumping and sweating away on top of her. "Enough, already. Get off of me," she'd say, turning her face away in disgust. If I tried to scold her about her selfishness and her lack of respect for my needs she'd let me stay on, but took the opportunity to tease me. "What's wrong with ya, can't get off yet?" she'd taunt, and before long I'd lose my erection and pull out. Finally assured that I wouldn't bother her anymore, she'd roll over and pass out, without even bothering to put on her panties. I often found myself wishing she had even half the heart that Kikuo had.

After that first night, Kikuo and I would sleep together twice, three times a month. Whenever he came over he brought me presents—expensive undergarments from high-end department stores. He bought me so many pairs they ended up filling an entire drawer in my dresser. But every time was just like the first time we slept together;

I would be on the receiving end of his incredible fellatio skills, and end up in stupefied bliss. Kikuo was fine with the lack of reciprocation. After I came and he cleaned me up, he would wait for me to fall asleep and then would go about getting himself off. Whenever he stayed over my place he would bring with him a fine silk handkerchief embroidered with cherry blossoms. He kept it tucked away in his bag. The morning after, he would always end up with a nosebleed.

"This is like my menstrual cycle. Sorry you have to see me like this," he said, stuffing the silk kerchief up his nose and looking terribly embarrassed. His body responded to gay sex with a display of a menstrual-like flow. He was certainly not a typical male.

Before long, rumors of our relationship began to spread among my bandmates.

"Hey, are you gay?"

"Shut up, you ass. I hate fags!"

We'd go back and forth like that for a while.

I had gone to great lengths to conceal Kikuo's nighttime visits from my friends. It was very painful and embarrassing to have them think I was gay. I flatly refused to discuss anything about Kikuo with them.

One day Mikio Yamada and his sketchy girlfriend Mariko dropped by the jazz band's rehearsal room.

"Hey, you're friends with Akika Wakamatsu, aren't ya? Do me a favor and introduce me to him," Mikio said to me as I was cleaning up sheet music. "I'd like to screw around with a pretty boy like that just once," he said. I was dumbfounded.

He was infamous at school for being a kid yakuza, for hanging with the wrong crowds, so I was shocked to learn that he was into both men and women. One time he had stopped by with a magazine titled *Bizarre Tales of the Sex Trade*, an S&M rag that had recently been published. "This is the stuff I like, ya know," he said, proudly showing off the magazine to the band members. He was into S&M, homosexual sex, anything. "I've been initiated into all the secrets of sex," he boasted.

There was a reason Mikio had asked me to introduce him to Kikuo. Kumiko had told Mariko that I was having a gay affair with Kikuo, and then Mariko spread the news to Mikio, resident yakuza member.

"Are ya a closeted queer?" Mikio asked, and I told him I wasn't gay at all. That's a relief, he said. "Kumiko will be relieved too, if you prove it by lettin' me have him. If I can get in his arse, Kumiko will be totally reassured, don'cha think?"

"Why the hell do ya have to go and do something so stupid?" I yelled. "Kumiko should've already cleared up her li'l misunderstandin' about Kikuo and me."

She had gone to Kikuo's house in Ikeda about a week before, determined to hear from Kikuo himself if there was anything going on between us. Kikuo called me to tell me what happened, and I was surprised to hear that she had gone so far. "I was surprised, too. When she suddenly showed up, I was so shocked I nearly jumped out a' my skin," he said. "I think I convinced her that nothin' was goin' on, but you should be careful. I'm sorry to be causin' you so much trouble," he added, sounding depressed.

I didn't know then how he managed to deceive Kumiko, but it was very odd to see how a woman could get rabidly jealous over another potential partner, male or female.

When I finally cornered the meddlesome wench and asked what had happened at the Wakamatsu mansion, she said, "I was so totally overwhelmed I ended up leaving without saying anything that I had planned to."

She said that when she sat before Kikuo in his expensive, splash-dyed navy blue *yuki tsumugi* silk kimono, she realized that she was in the presence of a famous female role kabuki actor, and she started to tremble. As she started to air her complaints, he just sat there quietly, with his bright, clear features calmly composed. His face was like a white cotton rose, she said. I was secretly impressed by the fact that she noticed his elegant and graceful appearance.

When I asked what he said about us, she replied, "He said that you were treating him like a little brother, and he ended up spoiled by the attention," adding that as he spoke his noble face lifted into a slight smile. After that, the noble Akika Wakamatsu treated her like an honored guest. He treated her to a meal of boiled eel over rice, then invited her to the recital hall to watch the rest of the stage rehearsal he had been working on when she arrived.

There were several effeminate male dancers dressed in wide legged *hakama* formal trousers wearing purple headbands. Kumiko said they were dancing wildly about the stage, so they were probably rehearsing *Yasuna* not *Sukeroku*. I had gleaned so much about kabuki from Kikuo that I was able to name the show from so little information.

One student beat a small hand drum as Kikuo, wearing a *suou* ceremonial robe, danced wildly on the spring grass. He apparently danced so well that Kumiko was enthralled by his fascinating elegance.

I think there may have been a not-so-subtle reason why Kikuo decided to perform *Yasuna*'s painfully beautiful love-crazed dance.

"When ya break up with a fag ya gotta let someone else fuck 'im. I'd be willin' t'help ya out, if you're in a spot. But it's kinda sad, right? If a fag gets raped he can't go to the police about it!" Mikio laughed. He finally gave up begging, but it was obvious that the rumors about us had spread like wildfire.

Also, it was obvious that there were students who were secretly—but intensely—infatuated with Kikuo. When we would sit together in the school's café other students sitting nearby would turn a laser-hot affectionate gaze on him.

Our relationship began to fall apart in the semester before I graduated. I've said it before and I'll say it again: I was basically heterosexual. My feelings for Kikuo were the same feelings I would have for a woman. He was beautiful and had a beautiful heart. But if a woman had appeared with the same qualities that he had, then I would never think twice about having a gay relationship. His face was like a sculpture carved out of the image in my mind of the ideal high-class female face.

But since I wasn't really gay there was no way that our

relationship could last for very long.

Besides, as time wore on I became increasingly aware of the suspicious looks that others were giving me. It pained me to know that they thought I was queer.

Kikuo noticed that my affection for him was beginning to cool, and he became increasingly desperate for my attention. I was planning on moving to Tokyo after graduating and working at a music hall in Yurakucho. I had landed a directing position there through a college friend. As soon as I told Kikuo that I was going to Tokyo he downright opposed the decision.

"A music hall's really just a strip club, isn't it. I can't believe you're willin' to work in such an embarrassing, seedy place. I absolutely refuse to let you go to Tokyo," he said, flying into a rage and scolding me in my own dorm. I thought it was far more embarrassing to be caught in a gay relationship with Kikuo. He insisted on taking charge of finding me a job after college. The Wakamatsu School was going to become a corporate entity the next year, with plans to tour abroad. "I want you to work in our office," he said. "I'll see to it that you get promoted to management level in two or three years."

"Fuck off! I can't let a homo like ya run my life. I don't want to be involved with ya that long anyways!" I shouted. Enraged, I slapped him across the face.

Kikuo fell from the impact of the slap and lay face down on the floor and sobbed loudly, his shoulders shaking. His pathetic sobbing made him seem all the more feminine.

The final blow which caused me to fatally resent Kikuo came a couple of months later. I received a letter from my acquaintance in Tokyo who had set up the directing job for me. The letter started off stating that "I would like to hear your direct opinion concerning the following matter." He was referring to another letter addressed to him in the envelope. I looked at the handwriting and knew right away that it was Kikuo's. There, in flowing cursive, was written: "I know that you have gone to great lengths to secure a position for our friend, but I am very sorry to say that after taking his future into consideration I must urge you to give up plans to have him work at the music hall." My friend must have thought that the letter was sent by my patron, and wanted to ask me directly what was going on.

I can't believe the little bastard went and did such a thing, I thought, feeling my blood boil. There was a major *buyou* school dance convention at the kabuki theatre that day, sponsored by Y Times with cooperation from several major corporations. The up-and-coming Akika Wakamatsu was scheduled to perform alongside several well-established dancers. He had begged me to see it, but I had constantly refused to go.

I thrust both letters into my pocket and stomped out towards the kabuki theatre.

The performance was sold out, and the backstage area was jam-packed. In the curtained private dressing room of Akika Wakamatsu sat several female fans who laughed and chatted gaily with Kikuo as he waited for his cue. Even the Souemon district geishas that barged in on us at the Taruhei restaurant near Hozenji were there.

Kikuo was slated to perform *The Dancing Maiden at Dojo Temple.* He wore a full, round wig that was piled high with glittering ornaments, and the fabric of his extravagant costume was shot through with silver and gold threads. His face was painted white, and he sat quietly in front of the dressing mirror. He was the epitome of beauty.

The sight of Kikuo dressed as the legendary Kiyohime was so stunning that I paused for a few moments at the door of the dressing room and stared, dumbfounded. As he placed a golden lacquered headpiece on top of his gorgeous wig he spotted me in the mirror and let out a small cry.

"Oh, you've come after all!" he exclaimed, his stark white face filling with joy.

In order to gain entry to the backstage area I had brought a small bouquet of flowers with me, pretending to be a fan. I threw the flowers at him with all my might. Shocked, he stood up and turned to face me, at which point I threw my friend's letter in his face.

"What the fuck do you think you're doin'? I'm not your plaything. I'm breaking up with you, here and now."

After I shouted the backstage area suddenly went into an uproar. The conductor for the piece came into the dressing room to wish Kikuo luck before heading out to the stage area. It was a customary courtesy between performer and conductor, but Kikuo couldn't respond. He simply stared in horror in my direction.

"I'll go to your place tomorrow around five o'clock. Let's talk then. Please, don't make a fuss here," he said sheepishly.

"Shut up!" I screamed. "Don't ever darken my doorstep again!" I said, and ran out into the hallway.

In a rage, I stormed out towards the exit. As I walked

I heard footsteps behind me. I turned around and was astonished to see Kiyohime running after me, the hems of her skirts fluttering out like wings.

"If you want to go to Tokyo so badly, then go. I'll become Kiyohime and chase after you."

Kikuo had told me not to make a fuss, yet here he was making a spectacle of himself, acting like Kiyohime chasing passionately after her beloved Anchin. I was scared witless, so I started to run away. I made it past the entrance, and Kikuo picked up his costume with both hands and charged after me. He tried to get past the entrance, but several uniformed handlers came over and seized him, trying to get him to calm down.

"You have to go on stage, sir! What are you doing out here?" the handlers said, forcibly dragging him back to the theatre. I watched them take him away as I hid behind a light post and tried to calm my racing heart.

The next day, after thinking things through, I called Mikio and Slutty Mary over to my dorm. It was foul play, but I needed a way to pry myself away from Kikuo. I decided to let Mikio have at Kikuo, right in front of me. When I look back now, I swear I must have gone insane. There's no other explanation for such a devilish, wicked plan to work its way into my head.

The final straw was when Kumiko sent me a letter saying she no longer wanted to date a pervert like myself anymore. This came right after I had discovered Kikuo's dirty trick that nearly lost me my position at the music hall in Tokyo. She had finally figured out that we were indeed sleeping together. She found out that Kikuo had paid to have a phone installed in my dorm. She also discovered my dresser full of brand-new shirts, socks and underwear, and learned that they were all gifts from Kikuo. "You're the queer's little gigolo, aren't you?" she wrote. Her letter made me burn with shame as I read each humiliating thing that she listed.

It was backwards of me to bear a grudge against Kikuo who had been so kind and supportive.

I normally made fun of Kumiko, calling her plain and artless, but as soon as she announced she was breaking up with me I felt a pang of regret. No, I didn't really care about Kumiko, I thought. But I knew that as long as I stayed with Kikuo I would never have the chance to meet an ideal woman. On top of everything, it made me feel like the scum of the earth to have people look at me thinking that I was a pervert.

I thought back to the ghastly sight of Kikuo dashing out of the theatre wearing his full costume. It was like Kiyohime had transformed into a snake and was pursuing me, ready to strike. I shivered at the memory. I felt that by calling Mikio to my dorm I was summoning a witch doctor to perform an exorcism. I had talked about the plan with Mikio the night before at a bar.

Mikio was excited to finally get the chance to mess around with Akika Wakamatsu. He brought along his weird girlfriend Mariko.

"Congrats. I brought a present," Mikio said, and Mariko handed me a bottle of top-shelf refined sake. I think he was congratulating me on freeing myself from my little gay shadow.

Kikuo was supposed to show up an hour after Mikio and Mariko arrived, at five o'clock. I opened the two-liter bottle of sake and got the party started.

"Ya can get drunk and then jus' sit there 'n watch the show. I'll show ya what gay sex is all about," Mikio said.

He looked up at the ceiling and said, "This place is sturdy, yeah? That's jus' fine," and pulled a brown hemp rope out of the bag that Mariko had carried in. I didn't understand what he was doing when he got up, tossed an end of the rope over the rafter and started tying knots. *What is he going to do, hang him by the neck?*, I thought, a little freaked out. "I'm gonna strip him naked and tie him up like he's on display. A li'l somethin' to liven up the party, yeah?" Mikio said, laughing. I knew he had a sadistic streak, but still I warned him not to go crazy. Kikuo was the son of a wealthy family, after all. "I know, I know," he said. "Jus' chill out an' leave it t'me." He hummed a little tune as he worked the rope into tight knots.

Suddenly, there was a soft knock at the door. Mikio jumped up, took Mariko by the hand and went and hid in the kitchen.

"Is someone here?" Kikuo asked in a hushed voice as he peeked inside and saw me stuffing Mikio and Mariko's shoes and bags behind the curtain.

Kikuo wore a white sweater and a scarf which he unwrapped as he stepped inside. He sat with a proper, straight posture in front of me and placed both hands squarely on the floor.

"I am very sorry for my vulgar behavior yesterday.

After the performance I reflected deeply on what happened. It was very thoughtless of me to send that letter to Tokyo. I offer you my most sincere apologies," he said, and bowed deeply. As he apologized he wiped away the tears that ran down his cheeks with his hands. He opened up the paper bag that he had brought with him and drew out a large, white envelope. On the envelope was written "Farewell Gift."

"I received a small sum of money as a kind of performer's fee after yesterday's show. I also received a fair amount of tips. All together there should be about $3,000." He wanted me to use the money to go to Tokyo.

"I can't accept your money," I said, trying to push the envelope away, but he insisted. "This is a symbol of my apology. Please accept it. It was short-lived, but I had a great time with you," he said, pressing the envelope into my hands. After thinking deeply all night, apparently he had decided that breaking up was the best thing to do.

"Also, I want you to take this with you to Tokyo, if it's not too much of a bother," he said, his expression brightening like the sky after rain. He reached once more into the paper bag and pulled out a thick, autographed piece of paper. On one half was the following message:

Farewell. I will leave sadness behind and continue to dance.
                                          –Akika Wakamatsu

On the other half was pasted a photograph of Kikuo arrayed in the dazzling costume of Kiyohime during a performance of *The Dancing Maiden of Dojo Temple*.

The picture was of Kikuo front and center, drumming a small taiko drum as he danced the part of Kiyohime, with several musicians lining the back of the stage. It was a magnificent shot.

"I'll cherish this," I said. "I dunno where I'm gonna be livin' but I promise I'll place it where I can always see it." My chest burned and my voice rasped in my throat. Suddenly, Kikuo threw himself into my arms, unable to hold back any longer. I wrapped my arms around his shoulders and held him tightly. He turned his face up towards mine, longing for one last kiss, when he noticed the rope hanging from the ceiling.

"What's that?" he asked, spooked.

At that moment Mikio and Mariko appeared from the kitchen. Kikuo, horrified, sprang away from my embrace.

"Enough chit-chat, y'all. It's our turn now," Mikio said, sneering like the boss of a group of bandits. Mariko had a cigarette hanging out the side of her mouth, looking the part of a malicious yakuza madam.

"Who on earth are these people?" Kikuo asked, turning his terrified eyes to me.

"Kikuo and I have settled things, so I want to cancel our plan," I pleaded, but Mikio's face turned red and ugly.

"I ain't gonna stop now! You're the one that begged me to fuck Akika Wakamatsu. I've been waitin' a long time for this! You wanted to see what happens when a fag gets raped, well now's yer chance."

Kikuo paled, saying, "I can't believe this." Mikio tried to pull him to his feet and ordered him to strip naked.

"How dare you! What right do you have to make me

do such a thing?" Kikuo said, flinging Mikio's hand away and clinging desperately to my knees, looking to me to save him.

"Hey, say something. Why does this have to happen to me? Hey!"

I just sat there, completely silent, with my arms folded over my chest. There was no point acting like I hadn't known all along what the gangster-in-training Mikio had in mind for Kikuo. I hated myself for being such a coward. I could do nothing but turn away, and desperately knock back the sake I had poured myself earlier.

Mikio once again tried to drag Kikuo away, but he started flailing wildly.

"Don't think that just because I like to fuck guys that I'm a softie," Mikio said, letting his inner yakuza shine through. He slapped him twice, three times across the face. Apparently he used violence like this whenever he wanted to break a woman's spirit and force her into submission. Suddenly Kikuo's entire body went limp, as if sheer terror had caused him to lose consciousness. Mikio tore off his white sweater, his trousers and his underwear. Kikuo's face went pale, and his expression hardened. His body trembled violently as he forfeited any resistance. Naked, he pressed both hands against his groin and shrank down like a sad little monkey. Mariko squatted down next to him with a look of intense pleasure on her face.

"You have the softest skin, like a girl's," she said. "It's really somethin' to see a pretty boy like you totally naked."

Hearing her teasing tone, Kikuo, mortified, wrenched

away from her and turned his tear-filled eyes to me. I couldn't tell if the gleam in his eyes was him cursing me, hating me or just sadness. His gaze was so probing that I panicked, looked away and drained my sake glass in one quick gulp.

Mikio took another length of rope from his bag and sidled up to Kikuo.

"Hey pretty boy, be good and let me tie yer hands behind yer back," he shouted. When Kikuo protested, asking "Why do I have to put up with this?" in a tearful voice, Mikio yelled "Shut yer face, I said!" and hauled off and slapped him hard once again. Kikuo was racked with sobs as Mikio twisted his arms behind his back and skillfully wound the rope into place. Mariko helped Mikio force the naked Kikuo to his feet and went about tying the end of the rope from the rafters to the rope that bound his arms. Mikio had said that he wanted to put the naked Akika Wakamatsu on display, and here was the result. Kikuo was right there in front of me, completely exposed. His face turned beet red as he tried furiously to wrench his body away from the ropes.

"Ah, and here's Akika Wakamatsu's dick. It's bigger than I thought it'd be," Mariko giggled, crouching down so she was eye level with his groin. Having a woman stare at his privates or touch him must have filled him with intense disgust and loathing. Kikuo tried desperately to hide his loins from her view by twisting away. He turned his flushed, embarrassed face to the side and let out a tense, high cry of vexation.

Suddenly someone knocked on the front door.

Flustered, I opened it a crack to see who it was. I cried out in surprise to see Kumiko standing there, something suspicious in her eyes.

"Sounds like yer havin' fun in there. Mikio invited me over," she said. Mikio noticed her at the doorway and called out to her.

"Kumiko, good of ya to stop by. Come in, things are jus' about to get interestin'," he said, waving her inside.

"You didn't have to go and invite Kumiko, did you?" I asked, furrowing my brows in protest.

"What's the big deal? Don't be such a snob," Mikio said, smirking. "Look at that," he said to Kumiko, pointing at Kikuo.

"That there's the woman—er, man, who stole yer boyfriend. Now you'll be able to get yer revenge," he said. Kikuo opened his teary eyes and saw Kumiko standing right in front of him. He snapped his head back and his body shivered as if he had reached the depths of pure humiliation. Kumiko was also taken aback by suddenly being confronted with the sight of the stark naked Akika. She couldn't hide her surprise. She unconsciously pressed her handkerchief to her lips and nervously stared at his naked body.

Kikuo, knowing full well that Kumiko was my girlfriend, seemed to be in excruciating pain. His face was bright red, and he thrashed his head side to side, writhing, as an intense wave of humiliation and shame washed over him.

Unable to stay silent, he called out to me where I sat in front of the sake bottle. His lips trembled as he spoke.

"All I wanted to do was to end things peacefully. Now I'm here, exposed and humiliated even in front of Kumiko. Why are you doing this? Why? Say something, please!" he said, a sob escaping from his lips.

As she heard Kikuo talk that way to me, Kumiko finally confirmed that we had been in a relationship. A glimmer of hatred flickered across her eyes and her expression darkened.

"Ah, but Mr. Akika Wakamatsu, when I went to your mansion in Ikeda you really pulled a fast one on me. 'Oh, no, he just treats me like a little brother and I let myself be spoiled by his kindness. One can't stop people from gossiping,' you said. You shameless li'l liar," she fumed. Mikio couldn't help but get excited by the fact that Kumiko had started to feel hostile towards Kikuo and spurred her to keep pouring it on.

"Yeah, you even made me sit through that rehearsal for *Yasuna*, or whatever. It was like you were tryin' to say 'Look at me, I'm so graceful and pretty, and I'm a great dancer.' What, were you tryin' to brag that you were raised better than me? You think I'm just a silly superficial schoolgirl? Well now I've seen through your dirty little scheme," she sneered, growing haughty and spewing venom in his direction. But as she spoke it became apparent that she had developed an inferiority complex after seeing what a beautiful woman Kikuo made. Kikuo didn't respond. His shoulders heaved with an oppressive sense of humiliation and he hung his head listlessly. He let out a small, weeping groan.

Kumiko, in a fit of desperation, snatched the sake cup

from my hand and drained it quickly. She was probably unable to mentally withstand, without the aid of alcohol, the intense bizarre atmosphere the room had taken on.

"Ya may be pretty when yer dancin' *Yasuna* but I think yer much more pretty standin' there naked with yer penis hangin' out. Yeah, really pretty," Kumiko barked.

Suddenly aware of her own arousal, she caught herself before the tears had a chance to roll down her face.

Mariko picked up Kikuo's pants from the floor and pulled out his belt from the belt loops and walked around behind his back.

"If ya go and steal other people's boyfriends ya end up facin' this," she said, and raised the belt high in the air and brought it down hard against his round, high buttocks. Kikuo gave a sharp cry from the pain and his eyebrows curved up pitifully.

"Come on, Kumiko. Here's yer chance to make this sad li'l queer cry out for mercy," Mariko said, and continued to lash Kikuo with the belt, each thrash cracking through the air.

As Kikuo's face reddened and he clenched his jaw from the pain, the girls watched him, shivering with an aching pleasure. They had completely lost themselves to the perversion.

I can't remember what thoughts ran through my head as I watched Kikuo being thoroughly tormented at the hands of two girls. I was so drunk I could barely form words. Maybe I thought I was dreaming, and the scene I was seeing involved complete strangers. But at one point I began to feel the stirrings of some deeply perverted sadistic desire rise up and give me the shivers. Many years later I would finally admit to myself that I was a sadist. I ended up as a writer of clichéd S&M pulp novels.

The source of my inspiration for torture and humiliation scenes was the sorrowful image of Kikuo writhing in shame as Mariko and Kumiko took pleasure in tormenting him. I found that kind of scene to be intensely and sadistically erotic. To my drunken eyes, seeing him stark naked, exposed, trembling and sobbing was like seeing Kiyohime entirely stripped of her elegant and extravagant gown and forced to bare herself before her tormentors. It was a bewitching spectacle.

"Alright, we can't just hurt ya, that'd be too mean. Now, girls, I want ya to jerk him off," Mikio said. Mariko tossed the belt aside and placed a hand on Kumiko's shoulder, guiding her around to face Kikuo.

Kikuo felt the heat of their lascivious, blood-thirsty gaze and was so overwhelmed with fear that he stopped breathing for a second and opened his tear-soaked eyes wide with terror.

"I won't let you do such a thing!" Kikuo yelled, his eyes filled with anger as he shot Kumiko a piercing glare. Kumiko glared back maliciously at the image of ice-cold beauty on display before her. The white-hot phosphorescent hatred that burned in both their eyes made them look like two women who were locked in a fierce, love-crazed battle.

Mikio grinned like a cat as he watched Kikuo and Kumiko engaged in their glaring contest.

He picked up the autograph that Kikuo had brought with him off the floor and shoved it in his face.

"This is yer pretty picture, ain't it. I want ya t' get worked up by the girls and come all over it. A picture covered in Akika Wakamatsu's love juice'll fetch a pretty penny. Ya'll make me rich," he said. As Kikuo listened to his cruel words, his expression stiffened.

"Kumiko," he said, his voice trembling. "I know that you hate me. Please, whip me. Whip me with all your might, till I'm dead."

"Ah, we can't have you playing little tricks, Mr. Wakamatsu," Mariko interjected, standing next to him and poking his pale, taut cheek with her finger. "You're so damn sexy when you're angry, Akika. It gives me shivers. That's why I really, really want to give you a hand job."

Kikuo's body shivered with a wave of humiliation. He turned his face, tight with shame, away to the side.

"Ya really hate the thought of havin' a lady touch ya, eh?" Mikio said, grabbing him by the hair and forcing him to face forward.

"Think of it as a li'l challenge between ya an' the girls. If ya lose, I'm gonna have Kumiko shave off yer pubic hair. Then, with yer smooth-as-a-baby dick we'll have ya apologize to Kumiko again. An' after that, I'm gonna stick my dick up yer ass—"

"Aah! No!" Kikuo yelled, thrashing his head back and forth as if he was trying to fling Mikio's hateful words away.

"How much are you going to make me suffer? When will you be satisfied? Do you really hate me so much?"

"Yeah, we hate you, we want you, we can't stand it!" Mariko laughed loudly. "Get to it, Kumiko," she said, rushing her along. Kumiko drew a deep breath, then squatted down in front of Kikuo. He let forth a piercing scream.

"K-Kumiko, please. Where's your female pride? D-Don't do something you'll regret!"

Kikuo's scornful words must have stung as badly as if an actual woman was questioning her femininity. Apparently it pissed her off, and she grabbed hold of his penis with renewed hostility. Kikuo groaned, despairing, and tossed his head back.

Watching Kikuo's face contort with embarrassment and shame, his face flushing red and his head shaking back and forth, made him look like a woman writhing as she was disgraced. I staggered over and stood next to him.

Normally I would have knocked Kumiko away from him, telling her to cut out this nonsense, but I had lost all human sensibilities and just stood there, transfixed. Kikuo's resentment and feelings of humiliation at the hands of my girlfriend Kumiko must have been painful beyond description. Just imagining what he must have been feeling set my sadistic desire on fire.

Kikuo's face was distorted with bitterness and pain. He noticed me standing close by and opened his teary eyes. Looking to me to save him from this torture, his eyes glittered with sadness.

"Please, for the love of god, don't let Kumiko do this to me. Make her stop."

I feigned deafness, and instead turned my gaze towards his penis that Kumiko was holding on to with both hands. Instead of becoming aroused, it seemed as though his penis had shrunk at her touch. Frustrated, Kumiko was furiously rubbing it, trying to get him hard, but Kikuo was so humiliated that his body showed absolutely no signs of arousal or pleasure.

"This is bad," Mikio said, noticing that the only stiff part of Kikuo's obstinate body was his back. "Let me help ya out a li'l," he said and walked around behind Kikuo, who kept on whimpering and crying helplessly. Mikio knelt down behind him and started kissing the high, round curves of his butt. Then, like he was splitting a ripe peach, he placed both hands on either cheek and spread them apart.

"W-What are you doing?" Kikuo yelped, and twisted and turned his body side to side in a panic, his face turning bright red.

"This is the best erogenous zone for a queer, ain't it," Mikio said. He wet his finger with saliva and slipped it between his butt cheeks. He groped a bit, looking for his anus, and once he found it he pressed in, rubbing frenetically.

"Ah, please stop! Don't do that!" Kikuo raised his voice in a shrill cry. With Mikio's help, however, Kikuo's penis began to harden in Kumiko's hands.

"Hey, let me help ya. I want him to come so we can hurry up 'n shave him," Mariko said, enjoying a shiver of sadistic pleasure. She knelt down next to Kumiko and started to play with his hardening dick. Probably due to a wealth of experience, Mariko's technique was masterfully deft. She rubbed a bit of liquid on the glans which had burst forth from the foreskin and wrapped her fingers around the shaft and pulled and rubbed the shaft. She lifted up his penis and placed her face underneath, lustily sucking and licking his scrotum. Kumiko watched her technique and copied her, also putting her mouth on his sack, sweetly licking deeply, up and down. These two had transformed into two lewd female beasts. I was impressed with Mariko's streamlined, expert manipulation. What moved me more than anything else was that Kikuo displayed a feminine and appealingly seductive agony in response to the trio's cruel ministrations.

His eyebrows were tightly knit, his mouth slack as he panted miserably. He opened his eyes, drunk with a thousand emotions, and turned them up to the ceiling. His lips trembled slightly as he muttered unintelligibly. It was the kind of behavior that one could only see in a kabuki actor that was trained for female roles. No other type of man would be capable of this kind of display of womanly disgrace. I even found myself wondering if it was all a show, the feminine fear, shame and embarrassment just him using his acting skills in a calculated way to release the pressure of the circumstances. His passionate writhing in agony looked like he was playing a character in a climax scene from a brutal opera. His own mind was no longer able to handle the intense pressure as himself.

As Mariko and Kumiko skillfully worked his penis, it began to show the stirrings of arousal, and soon expanded and stood erect.

"Well done, my pretty boy," Mariko exclaimed, staring wide eyed at the swollen member in her hands. "I can't believe ya were able to dance the role of Kiyohime with such grace with a monster like this between yer legs."

The muscles in Kikuo's neck stood out, strained, as he gasped feverishly. From the corners of his long cat-like eyes tears of humiliation spilled out and ran down his cheeks.

"Alright baby, we're roundin' third," Mariko said, and the girls giggled cruelly and increased the pitch of their handiwork. As Kumiko roughly worked him, Kikuo's face flushed red once again as he shook his head side to side.

"A-Are you really going to put me through this red-faced shame, Kumiko?"

The girls arrogantly ignored his plaintive cry and instead focused on coordinating their movements. They were in a trance of ecstasy. They were aroused by Akika Wakamatsu's large masculine erection and the smell of his feminine skin.

"Look, a li'l liquid has come out. Get ready, girls, he's gonna orgasm soon," Mikio said, checking the status of Kikuo's erection as he continued to mess with his butt. Mariko picked up the photograph of Kikuo and readied it for his ejaculation.

"I-I can't hold back any longer," Kikuo cried out. He had been suppressing it with all his might, but he was soon past the point of no return. Even so, at the eleventh hour, I was surprised to see that he still managed to show a womanly consideration for his tormentors. "Kumiko, your hands will get dirty. Quick, get a tissue or a handkerchief," he said, his breath a ragged pant.

"Quit showin' off. Yer supposed t'come all over yer pretty picture that Mariko's got ready fer ya," Mikio scolded him without breaking the rhythm of his anal massage. Mariko looked up at the writhing Kikuo with a gaze of intense pleasure.

"Here's the part where you have t'act like a man. Be a big boy now an' let it all out," she said.

"Make sure ya give us a sign when yer about t'go," Mikio said, wetting his finger again and upping the intensity of the massage he was giving Kikuo's enlarged anus. Kikuo gritted his teeth as his back arched, taut with tension. I felt myself being drawn towards the spectacle of his persecution, and stood close enough to touch him. I stared at his aroused, erect penis as Kumiko relentlessly worked him up and down. I gazed at him as he cried out crazed with embarrassment and humiliation.

We had slept together many times, yet I had never seen him reduced to this physical state. Basically, I was terrible in bed and was never able to get him off with my pathetic handiwork.

"After you fall asleep I'll quietly jerk off," he would say shyly. That's why I was intent on seeing him orgasm, unable to hold it off at the hands of these three people. Seeing the treasured son of a renowned *buyou* family reduced to a state of sexual helplessness aroused a sadistic and perverted pleasure within me. The sight of beauty and virtue being defiled at the hands of ugliness and corruption was a theme of the kind of C-grade dime-store erotic novels that I ended up writing. It's stupid and obscene, but the inspiration for that kind of scenario most likely came from the experience of watching Kikuo defiled by Mikio.

Kikuo was writhing furiously like he was in the throes of death.

"Ah, stop! No, don't touch that," he'd cry out, twisting and wrenching his pelvis this way and that. It was obvious that even in this state of agony he was thoroughly female. His mind and body had transformed from male to female. Even his speech reflected this gender change.

He gasped and panted feverishly, and his eyes, wet with exertion, flickered pathetically in my direction. He called out to me in a husky, spent voice:

"I'm about to do something very embarrassing. But I don't want you to see this part. P-Please, close your eyes."

I was mildly freaked out at suddenly being spoken to, and so I quickly averted my gaze and my eyes darted elsewhere around the room. He was apologizing to me, his lover, even as he was suffering wretched pangs of humiliation at the hands of his three wicked tormentors. Then, as if accepting his fate, Kikuo slowly closed his eyes, gnawed sadly on his lower lip and arched his head backwards. Sharp, intense pleasure seemed to radiate powerfully through his pelvis. His thighs began to convulse.

"Ah, I'm—I'm coming!" he yelled; his face, thrown back, was dripping with sweat. His charming beauty at that moment looked otherworldly.

"Yeah! We did it!" Kumiko cried, pulling her hand away from the head of his penis as Mariko caught his ejaculate with the picture. The two girls were wild with ecstasy at seeing his sticky white cum all over the photo.

"Aw, look, I got some on my hands," Kumiko said, clicking her tongue. She opened up her palm to show me that it was covered in a sticky film of Kikuo's body fluid.

Kikuo was so embarrassed he looked like he wanted

to disappear. His face was flushed with shame at having been finally forced to orgasm. He turned his head to the side and said to Kumiko in a ragged sob, "I'm sorry!"

I looked at Kumiko's palm, wet with his ejaculate, with envy. I hadn't been able to get Kikuo worked up to the point of orgasm even once. I was incredibly jealous that Kumiko was the one who was able to use her techniques to bring him to this place, to induce a state of sexual ecstasy.

"Hey, Kumiko's gonna shave junior's pubes. Don'cha wanna see?" Mikio called after me in a mysterious voice as I started to head to the door. "After that I'm gonna grease him up with Vaseline then fuck him up the ass. Isn't that whatcha wanted t'see?"

"No," I said. "There's a party in Shinsaibashi for the jazz band seniors who're graduatin' an' I don't wanna miss it."

"Ah, that so. I'm bein' held back again this year, so I've got it easy, anyways," he said.

Mikio jerked his chin in the direction of Kikuo's pathetic, naked, exposed body, drew close to me and said, "In exchange for ya partyin' I'm gonna take this kid. Ya don' mind if we use yer place for a few more hours, do ya?" He practically salivated as he spoke.

"The three of you are gonna thoroughly amuse yourselves with this little queer, ain't ya. Enjoy it while it lasts," I said, forcing myself to laugh. Kikuo had been hanging his head and weeping softly when suddenly he lifted his tear-stained face and called out to me.

"Where are you going? Are you going to leave me here all alone? Wait, please!"

The rope tied to the rafter creaked as he swung and twisted his bound upper body towards me. Even when he was agitated, Kikuo's movements were grounded in the well-trained gestures of a kabuki and buyou dancer. He was utterly captivating.

"Shut up!" Mikio bellowed, glaring at Kikuo's frightened face. "Kumiko's gonna shave ya an' then yer gonna apologize to her for stealin' her man!"

Mariko sidled up to me and slithered her arm through mine.

"I want to see what the dance-drilled ass of Akika Wakamatsu does when Mikio's screwing him. Ain't ya curious?" she asked.

I tried to shake off her hand as my gaze locked with Kikuo's, his eyes brimming with a glimmering sadness.

"Ya must hate me, yeah? This is the result of me bein' a bad person. I sold ya to Mikio, who can't help himself around pretty boys like' you," I said out of the side of my mouth. I stood before him, trying to make myself out to be the devil incarnate.

Kikuo laid an icy cold look of sadness on me.

"I will never, ever hate you. I was the one who was wrong. I never thought about you or your feelings when I insisted on seeing you. Everyone must've been really cold to you once they saw you with someone like me. I deserve to be punished like this," he said, as fat tears welled up and trickled down his soft, smooth cheeks.

At some point Kumiko and Mariko had changed into slips and were setting about preparing for the next phase of their torture. They had placed a bowl with sudsy water and a Western-style razor on a tray from the kitchen. The girls were completely absorbed in their sick, perverted fantasy world. They looked like they had been drugged, and they were in fact quite drunk. Kikuo seemed to have let his fear subside. He looked down at Kumiko as she whipped up a lather in the bowl with a brush with an air of cool disdain. Mikio, dressed only in his shorts, sat on the floor next to the girls, his legs folded and his posture straight as a king's. He slurped his sake with gusto as he looked up at his prostrated prey.

"After they're done shavin' ya, I'm gonna start in at ya. What should I use to lube ya up? Vaseline? Cold cream? I brought all kids of jelly," he said, then turned to Mariko. "Be sure an' wrap his short 'n curlies up in a piece of paper 'r somethin'. It's a precious item. His fans'll shell out big bucks for somethin' like that."

"Now then, Sir Wakamatsu, I'm going to shave you. Prepare yourself," Kumiko said, play-acting. As she sinuously leaned her body in Kikuo cried out, "Wait, wait just a second," stiffening his body, and speaking just barely above a whisper. "I have just one request to make of you. Will you let me have one last kiss with him? A farewell kiss?"

"Oh, sure, I don't care. We've broken up. You don't need to worry about offending me," she said.

"In exchange for that kiss you'll have to fully submit to our punishment," Mariko interjected, thrusting out her jaw.

"I understand," Kikuo said, and turned forlorn, tearful eyes to me. In his eyes I could see that this would be our last kiss.

"Kiss me goodbye. Kiss me one last time."

I wrapped my arms around his bound shoulders as he pressed up against me, his naked body reaching out for mine.

He leaned against my chest, desperately seeking my lips. We kissed long, deeply, and richly, our mouths melting together. After we finally pulled away, the look of longing in his eyes was so intense and sexual that it made me shiver.

"Farewell, my love. Please hurry and leave. I don't want you to see what's about to happen. Having you see me like I was before was so embarrassing I wanted to die," he said, his cheeks coloring with shame. He suddenly broke into a flirtatious half-smile. "Now, hurry up and get out of here."

Mikio suddenly appeared next to him and grabbed him by the hair, turning his face to him. "Enough already. Jus' you leave the rest t'me," he said, and recklessly kissed him squarely on the lips. Kikuo's eyebrows turned up as he grimaced from the kiss.

I felt like I was witnessing something I wasn't supposed to, and hurried towards the door. I got the feeling that Kikuo had given up on all hope and had desperately thrown himself into a cage of hungry, wild beasts.

I opened the door and stepped out into the hallway, but something tugged at my heartstrings. I felt a sense of incompletion. Quietly, I opened the door and peeked inside.

After Mikio released Kikuo from his kiss, Kikuo's face looked vibrant, refreshed, as if he had abandoned all tears and regret. He tossed his disheveled hair over his shoulder in one fluid motion and yelled, "Now, do with me as you please."

He stood with his long, slender legs spread wide apart, as if he was throwing down the gauntlet for a challenge. The whole scenario looked like it was pulled from the final scene of some play. He was dazzling. I thought about going inside and saying my farewells to Kumiko, but she was totally focused on spreading the shaving foam on Kikuo's pubic area. She was lost in a fantasy, dreaming of the next phase of torment they would pour on him. I felt that Kumiko had defeated me in the battle over Kikuo. She had stolen him from me. Longing for one last look, I turned my gaze towards Kikuo's face. Having thrown his body to the male and female lascivious beasts that howled for blood, he had resigned all emotion and gazed far off into the distance of some inner world. He looked like a statue of the boy Christ I had seen in a museum somewhere.

Late at night, I accompanied Mikio to the bathhouse. As I washed his back I noticed that he was so thin that he looked like a plucked chicken. We had talked a long while about the time forty years ago when he raped Akika Wakamatsu, but in his old age he really only remembered bits and pieces of what happened.

After the incident Kikuo dropped out of school. Two years later, after participating in an exhibition performance of famous Wakamatsu-style buyou dancers in Paris, he killed himself by taking poison. No one knew why he committed suicide. Rumor had it that he was depressed about not making it in European showbiz, or that he was severely depressed. Either way, I was deeply shocked at the news of his death.

"The reason he killed himself was either you or me, don'cha think?" Mikio laughed quietly, relaxing into the hot water. "I can't really recall much, but as far as I can remember I did some pretty awful things to him, didn't I." He seemed to be recovering some of his memories of that time.

I had left for Tokyo right after the incident, so I didn't know what had happened after I left.

"I was a really bad person in those days. I'm sure you remember that Mariko and I were into S&M. We took pictures of him tied up naked, pictures of us shavin' him. We made him into our li'l sex slave and had all kindsa fun at his expense. At one point, Kikuo lost his patience with the whole situation and blabbed about everythin' to a family member, even got a lawyer involved. I was forced to break off my relationship with him." He laughed bitterly. I had no idea that any of that had happened.

"They paid me $30,000. That was a lot back then. I had to give up all the photos and negatives I had taken of him. Thanks to you, I made some serious bank," Mikio said.

"After all that I slept with a whole mess of women, but I never met any girl who had the gentle, meek modesty that Akika Wakamatsu had. He was like an old-fashioned Japanese lady. If he was really a woman, I think I could have been real happy. Plus, he had masochistic tendencies. With jus' a li'l more time I coulda trained him to be my favorite type of gay," he said, sounding disappointed. "And he was really and truly gay. He hated women. No matter what trick Mariko used she could never get him off. I remember her getting so frustrated she'd end up in tears." Kikuo would be tied in a standing position to a post and she would put his penis in her mouth and frantically bob her head up and down, sucking like a woman possessed, but all it would do was make Kikuo feel absolutely humiliated and ashamed. "His face when he was sufferin' that disgrace was so weirdly beautiful that it made me want to hold him tight," Mikio said. "Well anyways, my time has come. Hey, maybe I'll get to see Akika Wakamatsu in the afterlife. If I do I'll be sure to apologize to him. Not like I can get up in his ass on the other side anwyays. Speakin' of which, his anus was amazin'. It was tight, with just the right amount of give. It was great, I loved it."

The next morning, I hailed a cab for us. I had wanted to do some sightseeing of the canyons in the area before heading to the train station. In the taxi we talked in low voices about Akika Wakamatsu. The Wakamatsu school of dance had dissolved years ago, and people's memories of them were fading away.

Eventually we came to the conclusion that his suicide was our fault. "Well, anyways, it happened forty long years ago!" Mikio laughed, as if it was all just a pipe dream.

"Oh, I almost forgot. This is for you," he said. He opened his bag and took out a large envelope. Handing it to me, he said, "This is all that's left of Akika Wakamatsu. Mariko had been keeping it as a cherished item, but she's dead now, too."

I opened the envelope and felt a sweet nostalgia well up within me as I saw the contents. It was the autograph that Kikuo had given to me as a parting gift.

> *Farewell. I will leave sadness behind and continue to dance*
> *—Akika Wakamatsu*

Time had yellowed the photograph and the colors had washed out slightly. The entire thing was covered in a fine film of dirt, so I had a hard time making out the trace that his semen left on the surface.

In the photo Kikuo was dressed in the dazzlingly splendid costume of Kiyohime, tapping a drum and dancing gracefully. Looking at Kiyohime's long, angled eyes and refreshingly clear expression, I was suddenly reminded of how clear and beautiful Kikuo's eyes were. I remembered how he gathered up that same luxurious costume in both hands and followed me wildly outside of the theatre. I remembered how desperate he looked then. I could almost see the conductor and hear the flutes and the twang of shamisens, the taiko drums beating. The sounds and images swirled around me like a vision. I could even hear the soft thud of Kiyohime's feet on the stage as she danced. I even heard him crying out bitterly, persistently, and terribly feminine: "I will become Kiyohime and follow you to Tokyo." The scene abruptly changed and I saw Kikuo, naked and bound in my dirty little dorm room. I saw him being defiled at the hands of Mikio. Kumiko was there in front of him, trying to work up an erection. His face was bright red, and he writhed in agony. His weakness and pathos that seeped out were painfully feminine. "Don't embarrass me like this!" he said, hesitant and shy. But Mikio was ruthless, and gave him no chance to struggle as he worked him further and further towards an inevitable climax. "Ah, I'm coming—I'm coming!" he clenched his teeth, gasping and letting forth a moan. The memory of that plaintive moment floated before my eyes, as if it were a dazzling final scene of some gorgeous play. The traces of his semen covered part of Kiyohime's face. It looked like the performer of the piece was having a hell of an orgasm.

I was drifting off in the glow of this particular fantasy when Mikio shook me by the shoulder and asked what I was thinking about.

"I was thinking, as people grow old and die, their memories die along with them. It's all so ephemeral."

"Yeah, sad, ain't it."

I waited for Mikio to fall asleep, and then quietly tore up the card and the photograph into little pieces, then put them back into the envelope. I felt if I threw the envelope into a passing ravine, I would lose the memories of Kikuo forever. Kikuo was dead. Mariko was dead. Kumiko was dead. Mikio would soon be dead. And eventually, me too. Did that mean the memory of Akika Wakamatsu and Kikuo Kazama would be gone forever from this world?

Deer Park

A CERTAIN LINE FROM A novel by the Marquis de Sade I read when I was young still haunts me. It goes something like this: "Hypocrites may choose to follow the path of virtue laid out in Christ's teachings. However, those who indulge in vice fulfill a necessary function of nature. Without vice there can be no virtue. There is no need for fear. One should stand in awe of the powerful role that immorality plays in nature."

The Marquis de Sade was under some form of arrest for twenty-seven years of his life for having committed various sex crimes. I never thought that having a bit of sadomasochistic fun with a few hookers was such a big deal. While under confinement, Sade wrote a number of intensely perverted S&M novels and stories, but in our corrupt world he could not put those sadistic urges into practice. Because of his deviant tastes, people discriminated against him, scorned him, and imprisoned him against his will. The resentment and anger he felt towards the hypocrisy of the church and society caused him to avenge himself by diligently writing incredibly perverse literature.

The Marquis de Sade lived in France under the rule of King Louis XV. At that time, France was overrun with sexually depraved, self-indulgent pleasure-seekers. The king built a small mansion called Parc aux Cerfs, or Deer Park, that housed several high-class prostitutes that serviced the nobility. Wives of aristocrats, themselves seeking pleasure, would pretend to be courtesans as well. Homosexuality among both sexes was common in the aristocracy. At the time, executions were seen as a form of entertainment, and were carried out in public spaces as thousands of people looked on. They say that a sadistic fervor swept through the crowds that looked on as a prisoner, accused of high treason, each limb tied by a rope each attached to four horses facing four opposite directions, was drawn and quartered. The sadism found in the literary works of the Marquis de Sade was simply a reflection of the sadistic nature of the times.

I resolved to build my very own Deer Park, an association for pleasure. It was about twenty years ago, and I had been plagued with ennui and an inexplicable sluggishness. I was worn out from getting involved with other people's problems—their messy love affairs, their financial troubles. I felt like people were no more than specks of dust or dirt, and tangling with them over each little drama drained my physical and mental energy. I felt sorry for myself. I knew a few people who were sexual deviants, and I was suddenly incredibly jealous of their single-minded devotion to pleasure-seeking. Their excitement about sex was contagious, and just talking with these deviants made me want to forget about the harsh realities of life.

Their feelings towards sex were innocent, pure, with childlike abandon and artistic sensibility. I say they were pure, but by the "normal" standards set by society they were viewed as perverted and impure, and their impulses were based on something abnormal. Yet I always thought about the Marquis de Sade's words, that betrayal and vice are necessary and proper when viewed as a part of nature. I didn't want to create an association for these devious types to simply study what makes them act the way they do like I was some sort of scientist conducting research. I was so fed up with the unpleasant realities of day-to-day existence, so bored and depressed, that I wanted to feel like King Louis XV reigning over my very own Deer Park. I wanted to be one of the deviants.

So I made a pamphlet to distribute to those who might be interested in joining me at my Deer Park.

At the top, I had a quote from Bakin Takizawa:

"All of the greatest achievements across a thousand generations cannot compare to the joys to be found in a single cup of sake. If you do not enjoy yourself while you are alive, you will lie on your deathbed agonizing over missed chances."

I wanted to explain that the founding principle of Deer Park was the awareness of the fleeting, temporary nature of life.

"So many people die having never allowed themselves to experience true pleasure. Many women who knew themselves only as faithful wives and men who knew themselves only as proper husbands leave this earth having never known anything better. They may have felt an impulse to act in a sexually deviant manner, but they never thought to act on those impulses, and thus died having lived a typical, boring life. Wouldn't you like to try living a life outside of preconceived stereotypes, a life that breaks out of the mold of conformity?"

I used that text as an advertisement to lure people into joining Deer Park. I didn't really understand everything that I wrote, but I wanted to express that hedonism can lead to new growth, new ways of thinking and ideologies. I tried to explain that having an awareness of the evanescence of life has brought people of this generation to a transitional phase where sex should be boldly celebrated. I hoped it would be an effective advertising hook.

I decided the location, the "mansion" for my Deer Park, would be the second floor of my house in the third district in Meguro, Tokyo. I spelled out the conditions of the Deer Park and gave an outline of events:

* Deer Park will be run as an organization limited exclusively to members.
* Only members will be allowed to use the salon at Oniroku's house, but members can enter whenever they choose.
* Deer Park's salon exists for the purpose of ladies and gentlemen who seek pleasure to interact, meet new people and discover new concepts through social intercourse.
* Lectures about deviant sexuality and love will

be held once a month by famous writers. We will also hold screenings of European S&M films, followed by guest appearances of Nikkatsu Roman Porno actresses, who will be available for casual conversation in a relaxed atmosphere.

* Bondage lessons will be held once a month by rope artists, followed by photography sessions.

It wasn't anything novel or original, just a high-class S&M club where sexual deviants could come together in a safe haven to express their sexuality and discover new people and ideas.

The enrollment fee was three hundred dollars, with an annual fee of six hundred dollars. It was a lot of money at the time, but I needed funds to cover the expenses incurred while properly furnishing the second floor as a salon. After all, I was soliciting funds from affluent types who didn't lack for anything. I wanted them to realize that S&M and sexual deviation was a form of high-class fun, a bourgeois entertainment.

I sent off the pamphlet to several associates that I was friendly with that had deviant tastes: professors, doctors, lawyers, corporate heavyweights, writers, actors, etc. I wanted to keep Deer Park limited to high-class members, and asked them to pass the info along to people they thought would be suitable. I wanted them to act as mediators, choosing people that, although sexually deviant, were trustworthy and able to function in society.

However, I made a huge mistake when putting the plans into place for the salon. Once I realized it I imagined and fretted about the outcome if things continued as they were. There were almost no women who wanted to join Deer Park. I figured that the men I had invited to join would come in pairs, bringing along their wives or mistresses with whom they were currently experimenting with S&M. I had even allowed women to join for free. But a salon with only men wouldn't become a place for any kind of meaningful interaction.

The realization (and subsequent vertigo) of this mistake was brought about by a certain woman, Ayako Masaki, twenty-eight years old. Ayako was the lover of Genjiro Kimura, an antique art dealer. He was the second generation owner of Aesthete, an art and antique dealership. He had recently taken over as president of the company after his father's retirement. There was a time when I was obsessed with swords, and I had met Genjiro's father through my sword-collecting hobby.

Genjiro, thirty-six at the time, had a wife and a child. However his wife had fallen ill and had been living at a hospital for over a year, so it wasn't unthinkable that he would have taken a mistress. I had heard rumors that Ayako was stunningly beautiful. I finally met Genjiro's lover, Ayako Masaki, on the day of a friend's funeral. My friend who had died had deep ties with Aesthete. When Genjiro introduced me to Ayako at the funeral home, I felt a suspicious stirring in my heart. She was handsome and graceful, and her expressive, solemn, sadly beatific features made my chest feel tight with longing. The soft line of her nose, her perfectly shaped lips made her beauty seem elegant and ethereal. The porcelain white skin of her neck which peeked out from under the white collar of the funeral-appropriate kimono was so fresh and youthful. She was a vision of pure beauty. My deceased friend had spoken of the beauty of Genjiro's lover, but in person she exceeded all my expectations. After I met Ayako, I made a point to invite both her and Genjiro out to dinner often. Of course, I was hoping against hope to someday have a chance with Ayako. I can't deny that I was aiming for Genjiro's mistress.

One day the two of them stopped by my house in Meguro after having attended a wedding reception. They were both slightly tipsy, having availed themselves of the alcohol at the reception. Ayako, with her hair up and wearing a black *edozuma* style kimono, was all the more bewitching when intoxicated. I offered them drinks, and as we sat talking Genjiro said they had stopped by to discuss a concern. I was dumbfounded when the topic of their concern was broached, since it dealt with their sex life.

"Ayako's too shy to say it, but she's a secret fan of your books," Genjiro blurted out suddenly. Ayako stood at the table, mixing a drink.

"Please, don't say anything embarrassing!" Ayako said, smiling drunkenly and glaring playfully in Genjiro's direction.

I write S&M novels that are intended to arouse masculine desire, so I was surprised to hear that a woman was an avid reader of my work. All I could say was "Really?"

"Ayako's a maso-, no wait, she's uh, she's a s-sadi-uhm..." Genjiro was so drunk he was confused and lisping.

Ayako turned her gaze to me, her wide eyes shining from intoxication.

"I believe I'm what you'd call a masochist," she said, her lips twitching up into a devious little smile.

I suddenly felt like a sledgehammer had fallen smack on the top of my head. Ayako's a masochist! Her words washed over me like a wave of vertigo. When a sadist meets a beautiful masochist like Ayako, the amazement and thrill are immeasurable. Sadists and masochists are forever fantasizing about their ideal partner, someone with faultless looks and a perfect body. "Have you known for a long time that you are a masochist?" I asked, trying my damnedest to affect the cool demeanor of a psychologist questioning a patient.

"When I was in high school I was gang raped by three thugs," she said. It was a completely shocking response and I had never anticipated it. My heart skipped a beat as I looked to Genjiro to see if it was really okay for her to be talking about such a private matter, but I got the impression that he knew all about her past.

"As I was raped by them of course I felt fear and humiliation, but I also felt a kind of masochistic pleasure, something I had never thought existed," she continued. She never pressed charges against those thugs, and never told her family about what happened. Instead, she kept in touch with her assailants and would occasionally go to one of their apartments to indulge in perverse rape-like sexual play. "You must think I'm a strange woman, to be friends with the very men who raped me. But I continued to see them for about a year when I was in high school," she said as she mixed a drink for me. She was able to talk calmly about the events as if they had happened to someone else. "Because of her experience, Ayako's not satisfied with plain old sex. Sometimes right in the middle of our love-making she'll grab packaging twine and beg me to tie her up with it. 'Be really rough with me,' she'll say, or 'Make me feel embarrassed.' I always tell her that I'm not into that kind of thing. I was wondering if you think I should have a doctor take a look at her," Genjiro said.

A doctor? I blinked dumbly at him.

"I had a friend once who complained that his wife's vagina was unusually tight and contracted so hard during sex that it made him feel funny. He had a doctor check her out. What do you think the doctor's diagnosis was? 'Sir, your wife has one hell of an amazing vagina,'" I said, but he was unimpressed. "That's not really the same issue, is it?" he asked curtly.

What Ayako said next was the turning point in the creation of Deer Park.

"But I think there must be many women out there who have the same peculiarity that I do. I mean, if there are sadistic men then there must be just as many masochistic women that can sate their desires, right?"

Without women, Deer Park would never be the haven for sexual deviants that I had dreamed of. Ayako was the first woman to say to me that she had abnormal sexual desires. And Genjiro refused to allow her to join Deer Park. "I'd gladly have her join as my companion, but I can't allow her to go in alone," he said when I invited them to join. Of course he wouldn't want only his lover to become a member. I couldn't say that it didn't make any sense. He was afraid that if she alone joined a club that subverted established sexual morals, the other men in the club would stir up Ayako's masochistic sexual desire. Genjiro was opposed to the concept of Deer Park, where nature was allowed free rein without the shackles of imposed morality.

He also feared the possibility that Ayako would fall in love with one of the deviant members of the club. Basically, he was jealous. Deer Park couldn't exist if its members held onto jealousy or fear.

However, I ended up feeling hopelessly jealous of Genjiro. I started to think odd thoughts. *Why is the perfect beautiful masochist Ayako with that boring old Genjiro? She's perfect for me. I should be the one to have her!*

Before long I held an opening reception for Deer Park. I figured that Genjiro and Ayako would show up to the opening party at the very least, but they never came. I heard from Genjiro that he had recently acquired a small gallery in Ginza, and that Ayako was appointed to an officer position in a new company, so I knew that they were both busy. Yet I had hoped that the dazzlingly beautiful masochist would show up and be the crown jewel to liven up the party. I was sad that it didn't turn out the way I had hoped.

Soon after opening Deer Park, I realized that the men who had joined came with high expectations of finding women to service their perverse sexual needs. I had invited several Nikkatsu Roman Porno actresses to dress up and mingle with the guests. I knew that none of them had any interest in perverted sexual practices, and I didn't expect them to be anything more than decoration. Their thinly veiled disgust with the situation was evident, but the men, empowered by alcohol, stubbornly persisted in trying to seduce them.

"Let's get together sometime soon and have a little fun. Are you a sadist or a masochist, eh?"

The men were all deviants and it was obviously a nuisance for the actresses to put up with their advances. It made Deer Park seem like just another S&M club. I felt ill.

The members didn't show any enthusiasm or interest in the lectures by experts on sexual deviation, or even the classes on bondage held by rope artists. But they were thrilled when a certain exhibitionist couple from Osaka came to Tokyo and allowed the members to watch them have live sex in the salon. They were Mr. and Mrs. Horikawa from the Daikoku-machi district in Osaka. They ran a dry goods store. Her name was Aiko, and she was just past thirty. She had the slightly rounded figure and charming features that men typically find attractive. Mr. Horikawa was the head of a wife-swapping club. They were deviants who loved the unusual thrill they got from having other people observe them as they fulfilled their marital duties. It was very rare to find a married couple with the same taste for exhibitionism, and I had made a practice of studying their live performances.

When they came to Tokyo from Osaka they stayed at a hotel near my house in Meguro. They called me once they arrived.

"If ya'hve got some free taahm, couldja come 'n snap some polaroids for us, yeah?" he asked. They wanted polaroid snapshots of their intercourse to peruse later. I hurried over to their hotel. I figured it would be rude of me to refuse their offer to display their sex in front of me, and so I thought of it as one pervert helping another. Although, I never really thought of that couple as perverted—I simply thought they were unusually open and free when it came to sex.

Or perhaps they thought of sex as a means to an end, a necessary part of pleasure-seeking that should be experienced in as many ways as possible. With a third party present, both man and wife were able to experience an even greater degree of pleasure. Mr. Horikawa was the head of the swapping club Crazy Dance which was popular in the Kansai region. It took someone like him, someone who found logic and morals to be incompatible with the pleasurable aspect of sex, to run such a club and to host boisterous orgies. I preached like a religious sect leader to leave moral restrictions behind. Even so, after I played around with his wife, Mr. Horikawa asked me to bring my wife along to one of our little gatherings so we could enjoy a foursome, and I balked.

"If I ever said anything like that to my wife, she'd divorce me at once," I said. I didn't think to apologize for my apparent hypocrisy, since I figured it couldn't be helped.

I felt a kind of hallucinatory effect when I encountered the Horikawas. As far as sex was concerned, they were illogical and immoral. When I was a young bachelor, I rebelled against the accepted morals and stereotypes set by society and behaved recklessly, but as I grew older I returned to the secular life, as it were, and had been tamed into living a simple, ordinary life. I was riddled with jealousy, regret and prejudice, and had developed the coarse worldliness that comes with age. The members of Deer Park—myself included—were nothing more than a bunch of hypocrites. It seemed like it would be impossible to create the pleasure-principle organization that I had dreamed of.

I even invited the purely perverted Horikawas to perform live sex for the members of the club. I thought the members' reaction was excellent, but Mr. Horikawa was unimpressed.

"Tha folks here in Tokyo don' know how t'party. They don' get inta it like the Osakans do. We invited 'em to join in, but they don' do nothin' but giggle an' look at us. With them all actin' high and mighty, it really kills the mood fer us, yeah?"

Mr. Horikawa had mingled with the drunken members and tried to invite people to join his wife-swapping club. Everyone smiled or laughed nervously, and ended up refusing his offer, he said.

"They don' mahnd watchin' a couple get it on in front of 'em, but they're typically selfish. They don' wanna have other people lookin' at *them* when they're doin' it. Sorry pal, but none a' these poor suckers is up ta snuff when it comes to makin' a hedonistic-like organization, yeah," he told me.

Each month more and more men applied for

membership. But all the men had just one goal in applying—they wanted to meet girls. I began to have serious doubts abou the future of Deer Park. The members all dreamed of the chance to encounter a woman who was a true sadist or a true masochist, but I myself had met very few women who were truly of either persuasion. Ayako may have been the closest to a true masochist, and I kept that hope alive. Sexual deviation is a priori when present in males, but it's an acquired state for females. If a sadistic man is able to lovingly and carefully "train" a woman, then she will begin to show signs of masochism. Therefore, it's unlikely that a woman will be a sexual pervert, but it is very likely that most women have the ability to develop a sexual perversion. After hearing the members constantly complaining about the lack of women I ended up asking the managers of S&M clubs in Shinjuku and Ikebukuro to send me girls. However, the girls had been trained to practice S&M for their jobs; they weren't true sadists or masochists.

One day, a member of the club who had turned sixty that year said he had an urgent request to make of me. He was a professor at a prestigious university. He stopped by my house alone.

I had a hard time trying to respond to every member's private requests. Not two months before, another member, a president of a foreign trade company in his fifties, came to me with a similarly urgent request.

I had invited Naomi Tani, a Nikkatsu Roman Porno actress, to the opening party for Deer Park. This president sang her praises, saying that he had been a fan of hers for a long time. I was fine with him going on endlessly about his critique of her films, but suddenly he became very serious, leaning in and saying quietly, "Just between you and me, I have a secret wish. This would be a lifelong dream come true." He rambled recklessly on. The whole desperate mess made me ill. When I asked him to finally spit it out, he chewed on his lip nervously for a moment before finally telling me. I was dumbfounded when I heard what it was that he wanted. This upright president of a trading company wanted to drink Naomi Tani's urine. He was willing to pay a thousand dollars for the dubious honor. Normally, if anyone made such a moronic request I'd kick him out immediately, but since he was a prominent member of Deer Park I couldn't just flatly refuse him.

"Well, I really can't answer for Naomi. I'll ask her what she thinks and then get back to you," I said, trying to dodge the issue with a smile. "You certainly have bizarre tastes, sir," I said, staring at the blank, expressionless face of the company president.

The next chance I had to talk with Naomi on set I mentioned his request. Surprisingly, she wasn't entirely opposed to it.

"Wow, I can sell my urine for a thousand bucks? I should do it every month. I can start a little pee savings account," she said. "Should I pee in a beer or juice bottle or something like that?" she asked, and since I had no idea I called the president the next day to ask.

"What are you talking about?" he asked, sounding like he was on the verge of tears. "You can't just drink it out of a bottle. Once urine contacts air it starts to oxidize and go bad. You have to drink it straight from the source!"

he practically yelled into the phone.

That's the way men who liked drinking women's urine had to have it, apparently. When I relayed the information to Naomi she got incredibly pissed off and said, "That's not funny!"

Here I've ended up talking about the trading company president, but that kind of golden-shower obsessed deviant is called "Nectar lover," or "Water Goddess lover." I found out later that it's generally considered a high-class form of sexual deviation. I think it's technically a form of masochism.

Because of that whole ordeal, I dreaded the request that Professor Furukawa, the law professor, had in store. Professor Furukawa was a distinguished looking gentleman with white hair that was slicked back and noble facial features. He entered the living room, looking meek and gentle, his kind eyes twinkling as we chatted about nothing in particular. Finally he got around to asking what he came to ask.

"Have you ever heard of Mayumi Kuronuma of Nagoya? I'm sure you must have, and I look foolish for asking such a question."

He was as polite as always. Mayumi Kuronuma from Nagoya was a dominatrix, a "Sadistic Queen," and practically a deity personified to men who were masochists. There were rumors that she was peerless, dazzlingly beautiful. However, there were apparently very few men of the masochistic persuasion who had seen this divine creature in the flesh. I was good friends with a Mr. Ogawa, who happened to be Mayumi's manager.

I had gone through him to ask her if she would allow me to interview her. I knew she hated mass media, so I made a point to say that the interview would be for my personal research only. Mr. Ogawa used to run a small club in the Nayabashi district in Nagoya, but he sold everything and left his wife and kids to become Mayumi's slave. He worked as her manager now, but his masochistic mind was still slave-like in his utter devotion to any work she demanded of him. He obeyed her every command and fulfilled her every wish. Whenever he was with her he would swear his allegiance as his mistress' slave. When he told me he even went so far as to sign a contract guaranteeing his slavery, my interest was piqued. I wanted to know more about this Sadistic Queen. I wondered at first if she was some sort of enchantress or wicked witch that had tricked him into giving up his worldly possessions and submit to a life of slavery. But if that's what a masochist like Mr. Ogawa wanted, then there's no arguing with his choice.

Mayumi Kuronuma also worked out of a high-end apartment in Shibuya, Tokyo, and several times a month she would commute between Nagoya and Tokyo. Her job was working with masochists who paid to be abused at her hands, and in her apartment in Shibuya were twelve such masochists that worked in shifts. All of them were men who had won her favor. They were rich, CEOs or senior managers who had money to burn. Each man paid anywhere from five to ten thousand a month for her services. With twelve men paying her so much money just to be walked all over, she was able to live a luxurious lifestyle.

Professor Furukawa's request was to meet the

mysterious Sadistic Queen Mayumi Kuronuma just once in his life, and to bow down at her feet like a slave. "It would be a great honor," he said. "I'm offering her three thousand dollars, but I would like for you to take a percentage for your pains in setting up a meeting." His eyes glimmered with supplication. Professor Furukawa confessed to me that he was intensely masochistic. But he was a gourmand as well, and took great pride in his refined taste. Therefore he couldn't possibly conceive of prostrating himself like a slave before a queen with any woman other than Mayumi Kuronuma, he stated. One can't really tell if someone is a masochist or a sadist based on outward appearances alone. Still, it was bizarre to see this well-built distinguished elder gentleman—a university professor, no less—state his wish to prostrate himself before Queen Mayumi and place himself at her mercy.

At the end of the month I got a call from Nagoya.

"Ah, Mr. Daahn. Hah are ya dooin?" Just from hearing his accent I knew it was Mayumi's manager, Mr. Ogawa. I had sent a letter to Mr. Ogawa about the professor's request. Apparently Mayumi had agreed to a meeting.

"Aftah readin' Mr. Daahn's lettah, the queen was reallah moved, ya know. Th' queen's been-a mighty busy ya see, but she was verrah pleased t' hear that someone thought quite so kaahndly of her. She says she'll go to Tokyo next Saahturday, ifn' that's fine with y'all," he explained.

I wondered if such a highly respected dominatrix really enjoyed having a manager with such a thick Nagoyan accent. Anyways, I was relieved that she was willing to come to the Deer Park salon in Meguro to meet with me and to work her magic on the professor. I'm sure it goes without saying that Professor Furukawa was absolutely thrilled at the news. He arrived two hours early for his appointment on that Saturday.

Mr. Ogawa pulled up in a Cadillac with Mayumi in the back. They arrived at my house right on time. Mayumi Kuronuma wore a deep navy velvet Western-style dress. Her beauty lived up to all of the rumors. Her cheeks were pale, almost bluish. She was tall and slender, and she had a refined solidness about her, like she was made of porcelain. Her eyes were a reddish brown, and showed a measure of sympathy while at the same time something cruel and merciless glimmered in their depths. As I introduced myself, Professor Furukawa stood stiffly at my side, trembling like a leaf, tense from simply being in her presence. I turned and introduced Mayumi to the professor, even though she and I had just met for the first time too. I held my breath as I gazed at her slightly tense, primly cold features.

"I apologize for my ignorance, but Ms. Kuronuma, are you only half-Japanese?" I asked, as we seated ourselves on the sofa and I found myself staring at her noble face. Mr. Ogawa blurted out, "What tha hell're ya talkin' 'bout? The Queen was born in Tokyo 'n raised in Kanda. Half-Japanese! What kaahnd a' fool are ya?"

He laughed about it, but still, it seemed like Mayumi's looks were exotic, like she was part Northern European.

Professor Furukawa and Mayumi seemed to be getting along quite well. As she opened up and became more talkative, he nodded agreeably and politely listened to what she was saying. She had the manners and bearing of a young miss of some wealthy family or even royalty, but I still had a hard time seeing her as the dominatrix queen she was rumored to be. As I watched her smiling gently and voicing her agreement with the professor's remarks, I tried to figure out where she might be hiding the sadism that made grown men weep with masochistic gratitude. I wondered if she really had what it takes.

The professor was trying his hardest to express to Mayumi his apparently unusual masochistic wish. His desperate attempt to communicate his desire probably bored this living deity of sadism. Perhaps it even made her a bit uncomfortable, but she kept a pleasant and slightly intoxicated smile on her face and didn't let on any hint of disapproval. She had the dignity and presence of a true professional.

"Ms. Kuronuma has to go back to Shibuya at eight o'clock," I said, trying to give Professor Furukawa the hint that if he wanted some S&M playtime he'd better get on with it and head upstairs to the salon. He was suddenly aware of the urgency, and fidgeted with the wrappings of a large package that he had brought with him.

"I bought this on a trip to England. I would like to present it to you as a token of gratitude for the chance to meet you," he said, and proffered a fine leopard fur coat to her.

"It has an excellent sheen to it," she said, taking it on her lap and stroking the spotted pelt like it was a favorite pet. "However, I can't possibly accept such an expensive gift," she added, trying to return the fur to the professor.

"It's simply an expression of my feelings," he said, trying to give it back.

"Then I will simply take your feelings alone," she said, refusing the gift. "I don't want your wife to get jealous of me," she laughed, trying to parry his request. "How about this. I'll wear the fur during our playtime. I'll be Wanda von Dunajew and you'll be my Severin. How does that sound?"

Professor Furukawa gave a small cry of delight as his face lit up with a smile. He was practically intoxicated with emotion. He teetered slightly as he crouched down, then prostrated himself at Mayumi's feet. Mayumi ignored this display, and stood up suddenly. "Shall we go and have a little fun, then?" she asked, smiling at me. She slung the leopard fur over Mr. Ogawa's shoulder and made him lead the way upstairs. The professor got up in a hurry, came over to me and held my hands in his and bowed deeply before scuttling off after his queen. He wanted to thank me for arranging a chance to meet with the queen who ruled his desires.

Before she went upstairs to the play room, Mayumi said she would wear the leopard fur and become Wanda von Dunajew. It was a reference to the famous novel *Venus in Furs* by Leopold von Sacher-Masoch. Wanda von Dunajew is the titular character who had the grace and dignity of a queen. "You will be Severin, the dreamer," she commanded him. The Severin in the novel is a young man who signs a contract to become Wanda's slave. He ends up on the receiving end of her sexual cruelty. In their contract was an article that said Wanda would appear wearing a fur whenever she would inflict punishment on young Severin.

As soon as he had seen them up to the salon, Mr. Ogawa hurried back downstairs to the parlor. He had told me that the queen absolutely refused to allow anyone to turn the session into a spectator sport. Plus, the professor repeatedly begged me to keep it top secret, so it made sense to let them use the second floor of my house in complete privacy. I let the other members of Deer Park know that the salon was rented out for the day, so no one would disturb us. Mr. Ogawa had helped Mayumi get into her dominatrix outfit. When I asked what was happening upstairs, he said that as soon as she was in the salon she was already in the work zone. She refused anyone—managers, pupils alike—to see her when she was in dominatrix mode.

Mr. Ogawa and I sat in the parlor talking over drinks. I wanted to know more about the psychological state of a man who had left his wife and children to become a slave. He scolded me in his thick accent. "What kaahn a' fool are ya. Someone who don' know nuthin' 'bout me can' understaahnd me. Plus, I'm-ah not so good at 'splainin' inniways," he said angrily in his moronic Nagoya accent, and wriggled his way out of having to say anything important. He kept calling Mayumi's apartment in Shibuya.

"I'm lettin' ya know where the queen is. She's workin' at Mr. Daahn's place in Meguro."

When I asked who was at her place answering the phone, he told me it was a young slave who was under contract. Whenever Mayumi left to work with a client she would have two or three slaves watch the place while she was gone. She would hold a raffle contest where the men would apply for the honor to watch her place. The young masochists that won would be dressed in nothing but black nylon underwear, a black mask and a dog collar. They would then set about cleaning the apartment, doing her laundry, etc., while they waited obediently for her to return. Each of the slaves would be assigned a specific duty, like cleaning the bathroom, doing the laundry or watching the phones. I could barely wrap my mind around the fact that that kind of masochism even existed, that these men would take pleasure in waiting for her like dogs. I suppose the pain of the long hours spent waiting in solitude was also a form of masochism.

The young men who applied to be her watchdogs weren't able to afford a real session with their queen, so in exchange for their diligent labor Mayumi would reward them by treating them like well loved pets, or would whip or spank them like naughty boys.

About an hour had passed since the queen and the professor entered the second floor salon, but I never heard anything like stomping feet or painful screams. After a while, Mayumi called down the stairwell, "We're finished." Mr. Ogawa sprang up from the sofa and went to assist the queen in getting out of her work garb. Mayumi changed into the blue velvet dress she had worn earlier and came down the stairs. She had finished changing while upstairs, and she carried with her the leopard coat. She laid the expensive fur carefully on the sofa. Her expression had barely changed from when I saw her earlier. The only difference was a faint hint of redness in her previously blue-white pale cheek.

"I just wore this for a while over a black slip and a pair of riding boots. Also, I tried this mask on, since he seemed like the type who would enjoy it," she said and tossed a silver bat-shaped mask carelessly in Mr. Ogawa's direction. He took the boots and the mask and tactfully arranged them in the black leather overnight bag full of props that he had brought along.

However, I was worried that the professor was no-where to be seen.

"He's still in a trance-like state, fast sleep. He should come to in about half an hour or so. Would you be so kind as to give him a glass of cold milk?" she asked.

I was impressed to learn how complex sado-masochistic play was, that someone would end up in an intoxicated stupor from the exercise.

Mayumi took a sip of the tea I had set out and said, "Well then, sorry to have put you to any trouble," and stood up to leave with Mr. Ogura when suddenly something tumbled down the staircase. I was shocked by the noise, and when I saw what had fallen I let out a startled cry. It was the professor. He had stumbled and fallen halfway down the stairs. He was completely naked. He took faltering, wandering steps in our direction. He looked like a skinny, wrinkled ghost. His eyes looked sunken, and his face was distorted with bitter sadness. "Ah, my queen, my queen," he moaned, and knelt at Mayumi's feet and covered her heels with kisses. Mayumi's face frankly betrayed the shock that she felt. She looked quickly in my direction and said, "It would appear that he hasn't fully recovered his senses just yet." The professor's pubic hair was shot through with white, and I was surprised to see that his thin penis was standing at full attention.

"Hey, professor, the play time is over. You look foolish like that, so let's give it up and go home already, shall we?" Mayumi said, crouching down next to him, stroking his hair and speaking with the tone of someone talking to a small child. However, it was as if his spirit had flown his body. His eyes were vacant as he said, "My queen, please let me drink your sweet golden nectar..." and tried to stick his head up her skirt.

Suddenly Mayumi sprang up, yelling, "How dare you! The impertinence!" She kicked him away forcefully. It was a shock to see the professor acting like a completely different person, and my shock was doubled to see Mayumi too acting like someone else completely. Her face took on a frosty, hardened expression. She glared down at the fallen professor with the piercing, heated gaze of pure hatred. Her eyes were filled with a deadly anger, and it made her look so fantastically beautiful that I couldn't help but shiver.

"Who the hell do you think you are? Don't mess with me!"

Mayumi drew close to the professor as he rose unsteadily to his feet. She slapped him hard across both cheeks. It was as if she was possessed by some vengeful spirit—even her voice had changed as part of the transformation. The professor fell to the floor once again, and as he rolled over he moaned, "Please, please, the fur coat..." in a delirious voice. Mayumi laughed a quick, nasal laugh.

"You want me to put on that cheap, sad little jacket? Don't make me laugh. You insult our royal person. I refuse your request," she said. She spat on the professor's face and then drove her heel into his cheek. I panicked and thought about stopping all this, but Mr. Ogawa was totally nonplussed by the spectacle. He just sat there and took a drag off his cigarette. At first, the professor struggled against Mayumi's oppressive foot, but after a few moments his movements turned lethargic.

As he began to calm down, she lessened up the pressure. When he was finally completely still she removed her foot from his face. The professor snored lightly. After making sure that he was asleep, Mayumi turned awkwardly to me and said, "I'm very sorry for the disturbance."

She seemed out of sorts. "Please cover him with a coat or something and let him sleep it off," she said, then hurried towards the door with Mr. Ogawa in tow.

I felt like I had just had a very bizarre dream and just stood there stunned for a few moments. After a bit, I went to the sofa and picked up the leopard fur coat and went to cover the professor. Once I got a closer look I grimaced. I saw a trail of sticky white fluid that led back to his penis. His member had shriveled up as if he had just finished having sex. It looked like a small, dried fish.

The male half of the exhibitionist Horikawa couple from Daikoku-machi in Osaka introduced me to a well-known businessman, Rokuro Yamazaki. Mr. Yamazaki was able to breathe new life into Deer Park, which seemed to be on the brink of collapse. Rokuro Yamazaki was fifty-nine years old, and owned a large construction company in Osaka near the Hankyu railway. Aside from construction, he also owned a real estate agency, a civil engineering company and a golf course in Hyogo Prefecture. His sons managed a chain of love hotels and gaming parlors in the city. He lived in Ashiya, on a fine estate that measured around sixty thousand square feet.

There was a luxurious Japanese style garden with a pond that held Nishiki carp. Through Mr. Horikawa, this grand master of business in the Kansai region informed me that he would love to become a member of Deer Park.

"He's a real big-shot businessman, but ya'd never know it by lookin' at him. He's a real nice guy. He's only interested in jus' one thang—S&M. He owns a golf course but he hates t' play. He says that all he cares 'bout is women an' alcohol. He's a bit of a weirdo, yeah," Mr. Horikawa explained to me over the phone. "He's got so much cash he can afford t' feed it to his horses. Why don'cha try an' get him to sponsor Deer Park, yeah?" he asked. If it has anything to do with S&M he'd be happy to support you, he said. I had suffered severe setbacks with regards to Deer Park. The whole project was going awry. Even if Mr. Yamazaki helped out with funding, all I could possibly do was to hire some pretty hostess type girls, teach them some S&M-like games and create a high-end S&M club. It was the complete opposite of my original intention, to gather members of the pleasure-seeking religion and have them spread the philosophy throughout the land. Mr. Horikawa wanted me to at least go to Osaka and meet with Mr. Yamazaki, but I just ignored him.

About a month later, Genjiro and Ayako showed up unexpectedly at my house. Genjiro was unwell, and Ayako's beautiful oval face was filled with sadness and shadowed with exhaustion. I set out drinks for them, but neither of them had their customary.

At a pause in the conversation, Ayako took the opportunity to ask, with a tone of formality, "Is there a member of Deer Park who might be interested in purchasing a painting by Gyokudo Urakami?"

Genjiro confessed that for the first time, they were having trouble staying in the black at his small gallery in Ginza. A privately operated museum had recently closed its doors, and when it shut down a surplus of ancient paintings flooded the market. Genjiro had purchased many paintings through an art broker, but easily over half of them were counterfeit. Even the paintings that were authentic had suddenly lost a great deal of value because of changes in the market. They had taken a serious financial blow.

They were doing well with Ayako acting as managing director, but just a year after starting up the gallery they were facing the very real possibility of bankruptcy.

"My father had a discerning eye when it came to choosing artwork. It was a mistake to think that I could fill his shoes as a second-generation art dealer at Aesthete," Genjiro said, sighing. He was fairly depressed. "I even made Ayako run all over town trying to sell paintings to raise some money. I've placed a huge burden on her," he said miserably, and turned pathetic puppy-dog eyes in her direction.

"It's no trouble for me at all. What hurts me more than anything is seeing you look so tired and worn-out," she told him, glancing at his face with damp eyes.

By the end of the month, Genjiro had to pay back a promissory note to a certain merchant. I was shocked to hear that the sum was two hundred thousand dollars. I had no idea if the Urakami painting could be sold for such a sum.

There were several artistically inclined members of Deer Park, but I couldn't think of anyone who would spend two hundred thousand on just one painting.

I told them I would do my best to help them out and then sent them home. After they left, I suddenly thought about the business heavyweight Rokuro Yamazaki in Osaka, who Mr. Horikawa had been begging me for ages to meet. I thought about telling him that a friend of mine, due to certain circumstances, was looking to sell off a prized painting. But then I figured he wouldn't want to go out of his way to help someone he never met. I thought it would be foolish to even ask.

And yet, if I managed to save the day by getting the businessman in Osaka to buy the painting, then maybe, just maybe, Ayako would reward me for my pains by becoming my woman. No, that would be impossible. But at the very least she might sleep with me, I figured. When a beautiful woman like Ayako says quite simply that she's a masochist, I couldn't help but think that she was my eternally ideal woman.

I got in touch with Mr. Horikawa and told him of my request. Just two days later he called me back and told me that Mr. Yamazaki had agreed to purchase the painting. I was dumbfounded by how easy this was turning out to be. On the twenty-fifth of that month, Ayako, Genjiro and I met up at Tokyo Station and headed out to Osaka. Genjiro had the Gyokudo Urakami painting securely packed in a container which he carried under his arm. In the train on the way to Osaka, both Ayako and Genjiro repeatedly thanked me for getting this business transaction settled so quickly. I couldn't help staring at Ayako's expressive features and marvel at her noble profile as she gazed absent-mindedly out the train window.

I found myself constantly wishing that Genjiro would disappear so that this could be a private trip for just Ayako and me.

Mr. Horikawa met us at the train station in Osaka. We headed off to Mr. Yamazaki's place in Ashiya right away.

Rokuro Yamazaki's mansion stood towering over the surrounding area, dwarfing the trees that lined the roadway. It was palatial, like it belonged to proper royalty. We were greeted at the entrance by a maid who led us to a broad, expansive room that looked out over the sprawling Japanese-style gardens. No sooner had we gotten settled when the sound of thumping footsteps came from the hall. It was Mr. Yamazaki. I was surprised to see that he was wearing a padded kimono. He was a large man with salt-and-pepper gray hair. He smiled warmly, and seemed to be a genuinely good-natured man. As we began to introduce ourselves, he took one look at Ayako and blurted out wildly, "Wow, yer a damn fine woman!"

Ayako wore a finely patterned kimono and an obi with a cloisonne design. Her hair was done up in a traditional "young wife" style which fanned out and framed her face. Mr. Yamazaki was utterly taken with her. As I introduced her as the wife of Genjiro Kimura, art dealer, Mr. Yamazaki said, "Indeedy, ain't she a fine piece of art." He was deeply moved. Everything seemed to be going well, until Mr. Yamazaki unexpectedly asked Ayako, "Are ya a sadist 'r a masochist, dear lady?" Ayako was stunned by the abrupt question. She turned to me for help with a look of timid desperation. Apparently Mr. Yamazaki wasn't satisfied until he was able to categorize every woman he met by their sexual preferences.

"S&M is my second-favorite thing. Sake bein' the first," Mr. Yamazaki said. "I'm a sadist, ya see," he told us, before launching into a lecture on his second-favorite subject. "Ya really can't tell a woman's true worth until ya tie 'er up," he said, thoroughly enjoying hearing his own voice ramble on and on incoherently.

We were all blown away by this sudden display of his rude nature.

Genjiro waited for Mr. Yamazaki to pause in his S&M lecture, at which point he stood and withdrew the Urakami painting from its container and presented it to him. Mr. Yamazaki said "Oh, right," and picked up the phone and rang another room in the house. "If Tatsuo's there tell 'im to bring my checkbook and come down t' the parlor," he said. Mr. Yamazaki didn't ask for Genjiro's interpretation of the painting—in fact, he barely even glanced at it. He seemed to be totally lacking any interest at all in art.

The sliding shoji screen door opened and a man, about thirty years old, wearing a suit and sporting a small moustache poked his head inside. Mr. Yamazaki introduced him. "This is my lazy son. No one will marry tha sorry son-of-a-bitch," he laughed.

"Write a check fer two hundred grand."

"What are ya gonna buy?"

"This paintin' right here."

"Uh-huh," his son said disinterestedly. Mr. Yamazaki tried to show him the painting, but he didn't care. He wrote out the check, signed it and pressed the family seal into it.

"This fella don't have no interests. Well, like his father 'e likes S&M, but that's 'bout it. I guess y'could say it's in our DNA."

Like father like son? I was surprised by how easily Mr. Yamazaki talked about his son's sexual predilections in front of strangers.

I marveled at the fact that such an open father-son relationship actually existed in this world.

Mr. Yamazaki continued to amaze; he was just full of surprises.

"I've got another son, younger 'n this one. Name's Torao. He's into S&M even more 'n his older brother. He's even formed an S&M film 'n stage Appreciation Society. Right now, he's out back rehearsin' their next show. He's awful excited t' hear that Mr. Dan was comin' an' I'm sure he'd be thrilled if ya'd come an' watch fer a bit."

Mr. Yamazaki took the check from his son and tossed it unceremoniously in front of Genjiro. "Well, let's go, yeah?" he urged us on and got up to leave.

We crossed the Japanese garden by stepping on carefully placed stones. We passed a man-made hill and headed towards a separate sukiya-style building next to a small grove of bamboo. It was a small two-room building about three hundred square feet in size that was built specifically as a rehearsal space. Mr. Yamazaki's youngest son looked to be around twenty years old. He was fair skinned and quite tall. He wore a beret and a jacket, and held a script in one hand. At the very least, he had the appearance of a theatre director down pat. As Mr. Yamazaki led us into the rehearsal space, Torao sprang up nimbly and headed towards us. He was different from his slow-witted older brother. He was affable and sociable, and when he greeted us his enunciation was clear and proper. After we were introduced he showed me the script that he was working on. On the cover was the title of one of my works, *O-Ryu's Passion*. Nikkatsu Roman Porno had just recently released a film version starring Naomi Tani. "The members of the S&M Appreciation Society voted for this to be our next project, so I adapted it for the stage," he told me.

"We're about to start the third act, where O-Ryu is attacked by her persecutors. I'd be honored if you would be so kind as to watch," he said and showed us to a raised seating area with sitting cushions that had been prepared especially for us.

"Alright, we're gonna take it from the top of act three, yeah? The writer of the original work is here today, so don't go screwin' things up," Torao said to the amateur actors gathered on stage as he slapped his copy of the script. I glanced quickly at Ayako, who had her legs folded neatly beneath her as she sat next to Genjiro. She seemed to be slightly nervous. She was probably wondering if the scene they would rehearse would touch upon some painful memory in her. Genjiro was quite obviously uncomfortable with this sudden unwelcome favor. He could barely sit still. I'm sure that he wanted to get away from this place as soon as he got his two hundred thousand dollars. However, he couldn't flatly refuse Mr. Yamazaki's request that we see the show, since he had come through and saved Genjiro at a time of great need. As I watched him barely able to conceal his simmering discontent I began to feel anger and annoyance roiling up within me.

Four or five young men dressed as yakuza gangsters in unlined kimono gathered on the stage. I was shocked to see that in the middle of the group of yakuza sat Mr. Yamazaki, reclining in a chair like a king on a litter, wearing a padded kimono. His son had cast him as the gangster's evil kingpin in this bizarre little show. Finally, from the wings came O-Ryu, her bare naked body bound tightly with hemp ropes. Three yakuza gangsters dragged her onto the stage.

O-Ryu's jet black hair was bound up with a coral kanzashi comb. Her skin had a rich, oily sheen to it, like the white of a boiled egg. On her back was her characteristic tattoo, which I thought had been expertly painted on in vivid, rich colors. I received yet another shock when I noticed that the yakuza member who was dragging O-Ryu along by her rope was the exhibitionist, Mr. Horikawa. I had wondered where he had disappeared. I found out later from Mr. Yamazaki that the woman playing O-Ryu was the owner of a club that employees of his company often frequented. The other actors were all S&M fanatics that he had met. I was astonished. Here was this group that could very easily become a respectable Deer Park of the Kansai region. It was a powerful blow to come to that realization. Here was Mr. Yamazaki, creating a little hamlet of pleasure in another dimension by simply bringing together his sons, relatives and business associates.

O-Ryu, pulled on by her oppressors, began to twist and writhe and fight back against the men. "Damn you, damn you!" she spat as she twisted against the ropes that bound her full, voluptuous breasts. As she staggered to the front of the stage her thighs parted to reveal a thick, luxurious growth of black hair.

As Ayako stared transfixed at the stage her breath suddenly caught in her throat. She pressed a handkerchief to her lips. A blush of embarrassment flushed out across her face, spreading all the way to her ears.

"Hey, dad, it's your line," the young director said. Mr. Yamazaki, who had been grinning like a fool at the writhing O-Ryu, got up from his chair all flustered and yelled out, "String 'er up, fellas!"

There were two lengths of chain attached to two pulleys on a beam in the ceiling. The yakuza gangsters set about fastening the ends of the chains to O-Ryu's legs. As they pulled her up, she was turned upside-down, her legs spread wide apart and her loins facing the heavens. Mr. Yamazaki the boss and the younger yakuza thugs all clapped and howled with laughter. O-Ryu's soft, supple body writhed in crazed agony as she endured the torture of being suspended upside down. Her lovely, creamy white thighs were twisted apart, and the muscles in her legs were taut with the tension of the chains.

One of the yakuza drew close. "Let's hear ya put some feelin' into that voice," he said, wanting her screams to ring out with even more intensity. He took a bamboo shoot that had been split at the end and brought it down sharply on her writhing, shaking buttocks. I looked at Ayako. She was pressing her handkerchief against her skin, which had become wet with a fine sheen of sweat. Her eyes glimmered as she looked piercingly at the stage. I heard her breath come in small gasps that made me realize that she was in fact getting perversely aroused by the spectacle before her.

Ten days later, I got a call at my house directly from Rokuro Yamazaki. He asked me what I thought of the rehearsal I had seen. I told him that quite frankly I had enjoyed myself. I told him I admired the fact that he had led his whole family on an endeavor to study a theatrical version of an S&M story so thoroughly. After talking at some length about S&M, he invited me to stop by his place in Osaka whenever I felt like it.

We were about to hang up when he suddenly remembered something.

"That Gyokugo Urakami paintin' is a fake. I had my friend Seisaku Kubota take a look at it. He's a professor at Kyoto University, y'see. I showed it t'him when he was over fer a visit. He gave his seal of approval. It's counterfeit, he told me, all the while laughin' 'bout it," he said strangely, then suddenly hung up the phone.

Astonished, I stood there dumbfounded.

I was furious at Genjiro. "That bastard. He figured

his buyer was just some ignorant country bumpkin and wouldn't know a real painting from a fake one," I thought angrily. Professor Kubota of Kyoto University was an expert in the field of Oriental art, and his opinions and judgments were well respected. He was seen as a living god by merchants in the antique and ancient art business. If the same Professor Kubota had branded the painting a fake, then I had just been seriously embarrassed by Genjiro. It looked like I had introduced a crook to Mr. Yamazaki, who had been so kind to me.

However, he ended the call by laughing about the fact that the painting was a counterfeit. He never raised any objections about it or asked what I planned to do to fix the situation. I didn't think of him as some sort of big shot, though. I just figured he was turning into a slightly addled old man.

I felt a rigid objection to Aesthete rise up within me. Or rather instead of simply an objection, I wanted to know how Genjiro was going to pay me back for making me lose face like this. I was enraged. Genjiro was absent from the gallery, and the manager who received my call was too frightened by my threatening attitude to offer a peep of protest.

"If the owner's not there then give me the supervisor," I growled. Finally Ayako picked up the phone.

On our way back from Mr. Yamazaki's place in Ashiya the two of us had secretly made plans to meet once we were back in Tokyo, but I never heard from her after we were back. I felt like she had betrayed me, and it made me angrier still.

"Oh, no, that painting was... Oh, I'm so sorry. There's really no excuse," she said in a terrified voice. She was obviously flustered. Hearing her sorrowful, puzzled voice made me feel a sadistic stirring in my heart. The thrill of it made me dizzy. Something unseen urged me to torture her further, to make her even more frightened. I started to harass her.

"I have completely lost face with this. Mr. Yamazaki might sue me for fraud. If you don't hurry up and come up with two hundred thousand, then things will get so out of hand that Aesthete will be completely ruined," I ad-libbed, a sadistic arousal raging within me. As I imagined her troubled thoughts and pictured her anguished face as she listened to my angry tirade I shivered with pleasure. The subtext in my speech was "Genjiro's no good, leave him!"

Suddenly I heard Ayako give a weak cry through the phone. A crazed sadistic itch ran all over my body as I felt an intense sense of satisfaction.

A week passed, and I didn't hear from either Genjiro or Ayako. I heard rumors from here and there that the Aesthete Gallery was in serious trouble. Apparently, not only was the gallery in Ginza in danger, but his house in Ogikubo had been taken as collateral. There were rumors that he had to take out a high-interest loan to pay back his creditors. Normally I would feel bad if a friend was in so much trouble, but in Genjiro's case, I figured he was getting what he deserved. It was all because he had tried to take advantage of the fact that Mr. Yamazaki was an uneducated country mouse and sold him a counterfeit painting in bad faith. I was also intensely jealous of his relationship with Ayako. I had developed a bit of a complex about the situation. Why was Ayako with him, when she so obviously belonged with me? I secretly hoped that Genjiro's financial ruin would spell disaster for his relationship with Ayako.

A few more days passed, and still no word from either of them. I felt an odd sense of premonition, and tried calling Ayako's place in Azabu, but she never answered.

Finally, later that evening, Genjiro called my house. He was pretty drunk, and he slurred his speech.

"Th' day after tomorrah, Ayako's gonna be back. We'll stop by yer place then, m'kay? Thank ya verry mush." He was drunk, but he was trying his best to be polite. I thought at first that finally they were going to announce the fact that they were planning to break up.

However, as I listened to his jumbled speech I began to put the pieces together. I felt my blood begin to boil.

Ayako had left by herself—without consulting Genjiro first—and gone to Osaka to apologize to Mr. Yamazaki about the Gyokudo Urakami painting incident. I berated Genjiro, asking why no one had spoken with me about the matter.

"You know what kind of man that Mr. Yamazaki is, don't you? Sending her alone to Osaka is like sending a rabbit to negotiate with a wild beast!"

"She's been there for five days," he said.

"Ah, this is really bad!" I said, despair and jealousy practically swallowing me up. Mr. Yamazaki would never let go of someone like Ayako. I had preached about the benefits of living a life ruled by freedom and hedonistic pleasure, yet I was choking on jealousy that seemed to come out of nowhere. The jealousy I had felt in regards to Genjiro had suddenly switched its target and turned its green eyes to Mr. Yamazaki. Genjiro was an unsociable quiet type who wasn't interested in crazy sex. But Mr. Yamazaki was like a wild barbarian who was only interested in S&M. On the one hand, I wanted a masochistic deviant like Ayako to experience sex with a full-fledged sadist, yet at the same time that was exactly what I feared the most. I was hopeless, just a typical jealous male.

The jealous indignation I had felt towards Genjiro changed to anger. "You've just sold Ayako to Mr. Yamazaki for two hundred grand," I barked harshly. Genjro was too depressed to fight back. "If that's the way it is then there's nothing I can do," he said dispiritedly. I heard his breath catching in his throat and realized that he was trying to stifle the sounds of his sobbing.

In the evening two days later, Ayako and Genjiro showed up at my house in Meguro. They were chaperoned by Mr. Yamazaki and his two sons.

"Sorry 'bout the sudden intrusion, but I'd like t' have Mr. Dan act as witness fer this here contract," Mr. Yamazaki said. He wore a black double-breasted suit. He settled himself in an imposing, dignified manner on my sofa and let out a loud laugh. It was as if the Al Capone of Osaka had dropped by for a visit. Tatsuo and Torao both wore black, well-fitted suits which made them look like yakuza guards that attended the kingpin.

Ayako had called me that morning to let me know the contents of the contract. She had sold herself into slavery, and Rokuro Yamazaki would be her owner. In order to release Genjiro's house from collateral, get out of the high-interest loan and pay back the loanshark's promissory note he needed one million dollars. Ayako's slave contract came at just the right time to save Genjiro from certain financial ruin. Genjiro truly loved Ayako, and so this situation most certainly caused him heartrending grief. However, since he was weak with exhaustion from his struggle to survive he wasn't in a fully present state of mind. I imagine that Ayako easily persuaded him into the contract with little resistance from the lethargic Genjiro.

In the contract, Ayako Masaki was referred to as Party A, and Rokuro Yamazaki was Party B. It read like a commercial contract, with some bizarre wording. "Party B reserves exclusive rights to Party A, both physically and mentally. Party A will not be allowed to have physical relations with a third party without prior consent of Party B. Party B will provide funding for Party A's personal discretion as well as security for Party A's entire life." This blasphemy in regards to human life was exactly what Deer Park should have been founded on. I simply didn't have what it took to run such an operation. I realized that Mr. Yamazaki, with his ability to place people under such contract without any hesitation, was precisely the kind of leader that a hedonistic pleasure-seeking sect needed.

"Ya think I'm bein' too hard on em, eh, Mr. Dan? Yeah, maybe I am. But Miss Ayako agreed t' this arrangement here," Mr. Yamazaki said after seeing the sour expression on my face. He looked absolutely thrilled. "Hey, give 'im the money," he said to Tatsuo. Tatsuo brought over a small brown overnight bag and dropped it in front of Genjiro with a thud.

"There's two stacks of bills, five hundred thousand each," Tatsuo said. I saw Genjiro start to shiver.

It was unusual to see Ayako in Western-style clothes. She wore a gray wool jersey dress. It seemed as though she and Genjiro had settled any private discussions before the contract signing. She had a refreshed expression, as if she had broken free of sadness or deep feelings for Genjiro.

"Mr. Kimura, do your best. Get your home back safely. What would you do if your wife was finally released from the hospital but had no home to return to?" she said.

Genjiro hung his head and lowered his eyes in shame.

I was moved by Ayako's genuine and pure heart. At the same time I was bitter over the fact that even though I should have taken advantage of the numerous opportunities I had, I was never able to have her. When I realized that she was about to become exclusive property of Mr. Yamazaki, I was filled with regret and hopeless longing. Genjiro was lucky. There was no telling how much longer he would have been able to keep Ayako as a lover, so he sold her for a million bucks at just the right time. If the primary message of Deer Park was to extol the virtues of immorality and sacrilege, then Genjiro had become a shining example of a life led by such values. I was angry that I had worked so hard for so long to receive nothing and watch him reap all the profits.

"Ah, I almost fergot. Since we've put ya through so much trouble, Mr. Dan, we thought we's leave ya a present," Mr. Yamazaki said. His son Torao brought out a package and started to undo the wrapping.

"It's a fake, but it'll getcha two hundred grand," he said. He spread out the counterfeit Gyokudo Urakami landscape painting on the table in front of me.

A year passed. The Deer Park I had created in Meguro eventually broke up. Genjiro eventually had to sell off Aesthete. He was left with just his house in Ogikubo. His wife finally came home from the hospital, and he spent all of his time taking care of her health. I would occasionally go out drinking with him around Shinjuku. Whenever we met we would reminisce about Ayako, who had left for Osaka a year earlier. She was probably under strict supervision as per her contract as a slave.

It was probably forbidden for her to write letters to anyone, because Genjiro said that he hadn't had any contact with her at all. The contract stipulated that Ayako and Genjiro were to act like strangers to one another, so he didn't have any right to ask how she was doing. "But what if she's locked up in some dark dungeon, hanging on for dear life as she endures terrible torture? I can't help but dream up the most absurd scenarios," he said.

"There's no way she's suffering like that. I'm sure she's living a perfectly happy life," I said, trying to cheer him up. She hadn't contacted me at all either. I was mystified by the fact that even Mr. Yamazaki hadn't bothered to contact me at all. If Mr. Horikawa, the exhibitionist, were still around I could ask him about the goings-on at Mr. Yamazaki's place. However, six months earlier, Mr. Horikawa had a heart attack while he was in bed with his wife and died on the spot. It seemed somehow appropriate that he would die during sexual intercourse.

Anyways, I couldn't help but wonder what kind of slave life Ayako was leading. My lingering affection for her still held sway over my thoughts. I even dreamed about her.

A few days later, I got a call from Ayako out of the blue.

"It's been a while. How are you doing?" she asked. Her voice was bright, clear and lively. "I'm sorry I haven't been in touch. Mr. Yamazaki forbade me from contacting anyone I knew during my year-long training. That training finally ended yesterday." She sounded so full of life.

"Are you happy?" I asked.

"I am. Very happy," she answered. "Now, to get down to business. On the tenth of next month Mr. Yamazaki will be celebrating his sixtieth birthday. He's only inviting a select group of people, and would be delighted if you could come to Ashiya to celebrate," she said.

"Are you going to invite Genjiro?" I asked, but she said mysteriously, "Well, after the birthday party there's an after-party—a Deer Park party. I don't think Mr. Kimura would enjoy watching me get gang raped by everyone. Since he's an old boyfriend of mine I'm sure it would rub him the wrong way," she giggled devilishly. Old boyfriend, she said. They had broken up just a year before. In just one year the Ayako I knew, so gentle, deep and emotional, had been transformed by evil forces into a wicked temptress.

"President Yamazaki keeps pestering me to call Genjiro, but I don't know, I don't really want to. He also wanted to invite you, which I have no problem with. I just don't think about Genjiro at all anymore."

It was bizarre to hear such cool indifference come from her lips. I think she wanted to tell me that she didn't have a shred of care left for Genjiro anymore.

I told Genjiro about Mr. Yamazaki's birthday party. He recoiled in horror, but I eventually talked him into attending. Of course, I kept it a secret that Ayako would be the star of the gang bang after-party. I looked forward to seeing Genjiro panic like a cat dropped into a bathtub. "They never called me," he said harshly. "And I can't possibly face Mr. Yamazaki now." He gave me a hard time about it, but in the end he caved. I'm sure he wanted to see how Ayako was doing, even if he was now little more than a stranger to her.

Mr. Yamazaki's sixtieth birthday party was held in the hall lined with white pillars on the first floor of the mansion. Ayako said that it was an insiders-only party, but it was a bit of a surprise to see just a dozen or so guests. There were women in Western-style dress as well as kimono mingling with the guests. I could see Ayako sitting in the corner, smiling and laughing with a middle-aged gentleman and drinking champagne. Ayako wore a luxurious silk crepe kimono with a design printed on the skirt and her shiny black hair was done in an elegant up-do. She had the dignified presence of a noble member of the aristocracy.

"What the hell is that? She's not a slave! She looks like the president's wife, for crying out loud," I said, trying to peer at Ayako while hiding behind one of the white pillars. Genjiro stood there with a whiskey glass in one hand, holding his breath as he stared at the charming figure of his former lover. Mr. Yamazaki's eldest son Tatsuo passed behind the pillar, his face red from drinking. As he saw us, he stopped and called out, "Ah, good of ya t'come, yeah. Next spring, dad and Ayako 'r gonna get hitched. A married couple with a thirty-year age difference. I wonder if it'll work out," he said, and burst out in a guffaw.

Married? Genjiro and I did a take and stared at each other. The slave ends up marrying the master? We couldn't make sense of it. Tatsuo called out to Ayako, who was chatting and laughing with some of the guests. He brought her to where we were hiding.

"Oh, it's so good of you to come. Why don't you come in and enjoy yourselves properly," she asked, her wide eyes gleaming with intoxication. She smiled gently as she led us to the head table reserved for the host and personal guests. Ayako and Genjiro exchanged just a few formalities.

"How is your wife doing? I hope you're working hard for your children's sake, too. It's good to see you looking so well," she said, as if she were a stranger totally uninvolved with his life. Ayako went around introducing the gentlemen guests as so-and-so presidents of such-and-such companies. Genjiro and I were so out of sorts that we could only focus on exchanging business cards with everyone we met. I watched Ayako as she talked and laughed quietly with the guests. I noticed anew her clear, black eyes and the regal line of her nose, the emotive features of her fine, oval face. It seemed as though her beauty had blossomed even more fully in the year that had passed. Aside from her cool reception of Genjiro she seemed to have developed into a pleasantly mature woman.

"Ah, so ya came after all!"

Mr. Yamazaki, who had been absent this whole time, finally appeared, pushed in a wheelchair by two subordinates. He was suffering from gout and had to use a wheelchair to get around. He was wearing an expensive casual-style *yuki tsumugi* kimono and had a blanket draped across his lap. He reached out to shake hands with Genjiro and me. He apologized for not keeping in touch. He explained that he took Ayako on a long vacation sightseeing all over Europe, which was why they couldn't contact us sooner. "I'm gonna marry Ayako next spring. I'll be makin' an announcement later," he said.

After hearing that he had taken Ayako on a tour of Europe and then planned to marry her, I realized that Ayako hadn't been treated like a slave at all; she had been treated like a princess from the very beginning. I was both surprised and relieved. I looked at Genjiro and saw that his expression had hardened. Whatever Mr. Yamazaki said to him he simply said, "Yes, yes," in a hollow-sounding voice.

Mr. Yamazaki surveyed the scene, then waved Tatsuo over. Tatsuo bent over his father's wheelchair. Mr. Yamazaki pushed aside the spaghetti that dangled from his son's mouth and told him that he was bored and ready to move on.

Tatsuo ran to the main area and announced the invitation. "Everyone, please listen up! We're going to head out back the other building where we'll hold a Deer Park-style party!" Mr. Yamazaki was a fan of the title Deer Park, and I had given him permission to use it from time to time.

The guests filed out of the southern entrance of the hall and walked through the Japanese garden. The moon floated in the night sky, sending down faint moonbeams that filtered through the bamboo grove. Torao, Mr. Yamazaki's youngest son, stood at the entrance of the sukiya-style building and greeted the guests as they arrived. He was dressed like a theatre director, wearing a beret and a jacket, just like the last time I had seen him.

"Are you going to put on a performance tonight?" I asked.

"Yeah, we're doin' a scene from this," he said and showed me the script he held in his hand. It was an adaptation of my novel, *Lady Red Rose*.

The plot was about a man who, faced with bankruptcy, deceives his wife and sells her off to a yakuza brothel owner. The man, tortured by pangs of conscience, begs to see his wife one more time. The yakuza takes the chance to torment the man by showing him his wife as she is being trained in the art of the striptease. The wife, in an attempt to relieve the man of his embarrassment and shame, tells him that she enjoys sex, and that she wanted to become a prostitute of her own free will. She does her best to look like a proper call girl.

I was worried about how Genjiro would react to seeing such a story played out, but at the same time I felt my sadistic side stir with anticipation.

Low, small tables were lined up inside the Japanese-style room. On the tables were sake bottles and an assortment of appetizers. Mr. Yamazaki had his escorts carry him into the room, wheelchair and all, and sat him near the alcove. Ayako hurried into the room, headed towards Mr. Yamazaki, sat down with folded legs beneath her and bowed her head deeply to the guests.

Tatsuo stood next to them and faced the guests. "I am very pleased to announce that my father, Rokuro Yamazaki, and Ayako Masaki are engaged," he said. All at once, the guests burst into applause.

"Yeah, you go you lady-killer!"

"Dirty ol' man!"

"King of deviants!"

The guests hooted and hollered, heckling Mr. Yamazaki, but he just sat there pleasantly smiling and nodding like a happy Buddha.

"Well, because of this I'm sorry t' say that tonight will be the last time that Ayako will perform with the Deer Park Ensemble," Mr. Yamazaki said and the crowd answered by booing him. All of the dozen or so guests that were at the party were members of the Osaka Deer Park run by Mr. Yamazaki.

"Don't be whinin' none. Since it's her last show as a sex slave, we're gonna make her work hard!"

Genjiro, sitting next to me, suddenly gulped back his sake in a fit of desperation. "The perverts, the damn twisted bastards," he muttered in a low voice, as if he was trying to put a curse on them. He was probably relying on the strength of the alcohol to try and drink away the bizarre feeling of wandering around in this strange, warped dimension.

Torao, in his beret and jacket, hurried about the room placing old paper lanterns and shamisens in the middle of the guests who were seated in a circle. He then hurried over to Ayako who was pouring another serving of sake for Mr. Yamazaki.

"Alright, mother. We're ready fer yer prologue," he said.

"What prologue?" his father asked his director son, looking very puzzled.

"I was gonna start with mother doing a Japanese *buyou* dance. I figured we'd start the play once th' guests were settled—"

"What are ya, stupid? Cut that borin' crap out."

"Okay. Mother, we'll start with th' scene where ya take off yer kimono, then," Torao said to Ayako. He hastily exchanged the props he had placed in the middle of the floor. I was floored to hear Mr. Yamazaki's two sons refer to Ayako, just barely in her thirties, as "mother" simply because she was engaged to their father.

Three of the Deer Park members, dressed as thugs, moved slowly through the crowd towards the playing area. They were apparently the same men who had played yakuza gangsters in *O-Ryu's Passion*.

Eventually, Ayako got up and slipped through the crowd. She slid sideways into a position on the floor surrounded by the three thugs. Suddenly a middle-aged woman in a white apron hurried over and combed her black hair out of its up-do. Ayako's hair was teased out and tumbled loosely about her cheeks. I was surprised to see that they had hired an actual hair and make-up artist.

I was further surprised to watch the make-up lady rip open the collar of Ayako's expensive *susomoyo* kimono and expose the hem of the light-colored undergarment beneath. The make-up artist worked quickly and suddenly Ayako's ivory colored calves were clearly exposed. I think she was going for the look of the character in a state of serene contemplation after she violently tried to resist the yakuza but ended up dragged to their feet. It was a tragic image of a woman broken like a fallen flower.

"This scene is where the wife is forced to repay her husband's debts by taking off her clothes," Torao explained to the crowd. A member of the troupe was serving sake to a guest, who was bowing and saying, "Thank you, thank you so much." Torao grabbed him by the collar and dragged him back towards the playing area.

"Alright, music please!" Torao said, signaling the conductor in the hallway. The room suddenly filled with the intro to "Besame Mucho." "You idiot, this ain't a strip show!" the director yelled, and then the song changed to a slow, melancholic melody.

Ayako stood there quietly with her eyes closed for a moment, getting into character. Then, she slowly opened her eyes and said, "You want me to strip off my kimono? Very well, then."

She stood tall and resolute as she placed both hands on her obi. She slowly untied the string on the obi, then undid the sash that held the obi in place. Her pale fingers trembled as she unwound the many strings that wrapped around the waist of the kimono. As she finally began to unwrap the obi itself, the drunken party guests were further intoxicated by this display.

Genjiro could barely contain himself.

"Why does she have to embarrass herself in front of everyone like this? I can't figure out what the hell's going on in her head," he whispered, his voice rasping in my ear.

There was no point in trying to explain to him that a sadistic male enjoys torturing a woman by embarrassing her, and a masochistic female enjoys being embarrassed at the hands of a male. I abandoned him and his anxiety and sat staring, entranced by Ayako's sexiness.

She let the obi slip to the floor. She shrugged off the pale purple kimono with a delicate bamboo pattern and let it fall away. She stood there in her charming under-kimono which was pale blue and had a small detailed pattern.

The thugs began to yell. "Take it all off!" "Yeah, take off yer loincloth too!" "Ya gotta get totally naked! Show us yer pussy!"

I think Torao was trying to direct the scene to show the woman writhing in agonized shame as the wild beast-like men shouted at her.

Sobbing softly, Ayako undid the under-kimono and let it drop. Then she removed the white Japanese-style slip and stood there exposed, her pale skin shining like porcelain. I gulped hard as I looked at her perfect, round breasts that seemed to be nearly bursting with fullness. Without thinking, Ayako wrapped her arms around her breasts. She writhed, driven to distraction with shame, and tried to bend over to cover herself up.

"Hey, ya better hurry up and take off yer loincloth, too! Ya gotta strip naked!" the thugs yelled pressing in threateningly.

Ayako pressed her hand firmly against the single cord

that held her pale blue loincloth in place, the single layer of clothing that still covered the lower part of her body.

"Please," she said. "Let me keep this shred of dignity." She shook her head violently back and forth.

"No, no way! We wanna see your pussy!" the thugs said, drawing in closer, and tried to tear off the loincloth. This scene, where the men and their captive woman battled over the last bit of clothing, was the kind of eroticism that Mr. Yamazaki liked. He sat there in a daze with his jaw slack, stunned by the display of pure voluptuousness. He stared with a demented look in his eyes.

Finally they stripped off her loincloth. Ayako fell to the floor, naked and sobbing. The thugs turned her over and lifted up her torso. Ayako tried to hide her crotch from the lascivious stares of the thugs by covering it with her hands and twisting her hips away. The thugs snarled and clicked their tongues in disapproval at her last attempt at resistance.

"Alright, if yer gonna act like that then we're gonna tie ya up so ya can't move. We can't have ya tryin' to cover up that pretty pussy."

The men twisted her arms behind her back and tightly wound a rope around her. Ayako, resigned to defeat, lifted up her face; it was covered in her disheveled, tangled hair. She prostrated herself before the men, blinked her eyes sadly and faced the crowd. She let the men do with her as they pleased.

"Okay then, get up," one of the thugs said and heaved her up by the end of the rope. She teetered and looked as though she might fall forward. The audience burst into applause at the sight of her perfectly symmetrical ivory white naked body bound up by ropes.

As I stared at Ayako standing there naked right in front of me I felt a slow-burning intoxication wend its way through my entire body. The hemp rope pressed tightly into her flesh, pushing up her fantastic breasts like two round, white peaches. The folds of the flesh of her groin were seductive. The slender shape of her calves and thighs were like the long, beautiful lines of a dancer's legs. The light shone on her milky white thighs, and her pubic area was covered warmly with jet-black well-shaped curls. I was shaken to the core, and an erotic ache began to throb in me. Ayako's face was flushed red with a stifling embarrassment. She turned her head to the side, clenching her jaw and bearing up under the weight of shame. They had reached the climax of the performance. Normally a simple scene where a woman is forced to undress would hardly be enough for a full-fledged S&M show. But because Ayako was stunningly beautiful and had a flawlessly elegant body, this was more than enough for the deviant crowd of onlookers.

"Hey, what's wrong? Are you ill?" I asked Genjiro, who had slumped over in a drunken slumber. I shook him by the shoulder. I figured it was easier for him to pretend to be asleep with Ayako standing naked in front of everyone. He was probably maddened by the fact that those sensitive, perfect breasts, that smooth, charming belly, those full and voluptuous thighs and that meltingly soft patch of black curls were all once his possessions. He was obviously tortured by this event.

He couldn't bear to watch, so all he could do was to pretend to have fallen asleep from drinking too much.

I looked up and saw that out of nowhere the floor was covered with blankets and pillows. The male and female guests pressed in towards the middle, cheering and crying out in delight. Mr. Yamazaki dragged himself into the throng and repeatedly waved to me to get me to join in. I left Genjiro behind in his fake drunken slumber and wriggled into the crowd. As I reached a place where I could look into the middle, I cried out in surprise at what I saw. There on the floor on top of a pile of bedding, Ayako, still tied up, was getting screwed by two naked men. The men covered her breasts, thighs, every part of her with kisses. She writhed and strained against the ropes that bound her. I was taken aback to notice that the two men were none other than Mr. Yamazaki's sons.

Ayako panted as they held her tightly. The younger brother sat with his legs stretched out on the blankets. Ayako straddled Torao, and the elder brother helped spread her thighs wide. Their legs interlocked, their private parts mingling; they rocked their hips back and forth, panting feverishly. Torao held Ayako's well-muscled buttocks in both hands, supporting her. He pulled her hips closer, then pushed her away, enjoying the rhythm of the undulating movement. Tatsuo ran his hands down her back and stroked her butt. He pressed against her back and nuzzled against her red hot cheek. "How does that feel, mother? Does it feel good?" he asked.

"Yes, it feels really good. I think I'm gonna come," she said, her breath coming in ragged gasps. Mr. Yamazaki stared at them with a devilish gleam in his eyes.

"I don' care if Ayako comes, but Torao, son, ya better pull out if ya fell yer gonna spew. It'd be hard to explain t' the neighbors how my wife got knocked up by my son!" he said.

The guests burst out into loud laughter as they watched the sexual display in front of them.

I was absolutely floored. How could this man let his fiancée get screwed by two other men, by his sons, no less? I figured he was either a genius or just flat-out insane. I wondered if Mr. Yamazaki was impotent, and decided to satisfy his wife's sexual needs by using the two people he trusted more than anyone else on this earth. I thought it was strange enough that there was a father who was foolish enough to brag to other people about the fact that his sons shared the same enthusiasm for S&M as he did. At the same time, I thought it was admirable that as a father he was willing to shatter the concepts of traditional morality. Perhaps it was only possible because he was tenacious and successful, and traditional self-denying morality went against his nature. Perhaps he felt that people were most true to natural law when they lived a life of pure pleasure and ignored the antagonistic forces of tradition, custom and morality.

I noticed that an odd mood had flooded the room. The men and women who were staring transfixed at the sex show before them began to unconsciously undress. Women stripped off their blouses and their gentlemen counterparts rubbed their breasts. Couples collapsed into heaps on the floor. Some women lay on their backs and helped their men out of their trousers and underwear. They took the men's erect penises into their mouths. Men who didn't have a female companion stripped off their pants and underwear by themselves and started masturbating, staring at the scene around them with bloodshot eyes. Mr. Yamazaki made his way back towards his wheelchair where an assistant poured more sake for him. He looked around with satisfaction at the orgy. I noticed that he had lifted the hem of his kimono up and exposed his genitals. A woman sat next to him, trying to work him up with her hands, but his penis refused to harden. Mr. Yamazaki didn't seem to care—he sat there singing strangely "Pee-pee, pussy, pee-pee, pussy," in a drunken stupor.

Ayako and Torao were getting closer to an orgasm. They were absorbed in a storm of white-hot sexual heat. Their hips rocked and rolled, undulating violently. Ayako tossed her disheveled hair over her shoulder as she panted in short, hot gasps. She pressed her lips firmly against Torao's. Suddenly he arched his back and tried to pull away from Ayako.

"W-What's wrong, Torao?"

"I'm gonna come!"

"It's okay, just keep going. Don't worry about it."

"Really? Can I?"

"Yeah, I'm going to come with you."

They greedily devoured each other's lips and tongue. Their bodies trembled as they neared the sweet release of a climax.

Torao collapsed on the bedding, completely exhausted.

Ayako didn't give herself any time to wallow in the pleasant afterglow. She turned her bedroom eyes to Tatsuo, who held her by the shoulders, and kissed him on the lips.

"You always like fellatio. Here, I'll start right away," she said. She suddenly seemed like a beautiful young mother who was looking after two mischievous young sons. With her arms still bound behind her, she sat up straight on the bedding. Tatsuo faced her and proudly stuck out his sturdy, engorged penis right in front of her nose, like a naughty boy playing a prank.

"Tatsuo, yours is so big! It's very nice, but I wonder if I can fit it all in my mouth," Ayako whispered sweetly, rubbing her lips lightly against the head of his penis, which was red and swollen. Tatsuo thrust his pelvis out impatiently.

"Come on, suck me off, mother."

I suddenly shivered violently as if a vengeful ghost had latched onto my body. Mr. Yamazaki had married and divorced several times, and his sons were victims of a severely perverted Oedipus complex. Their father must have noticed. "Mothers these days don' know how t' talk to their kids 'bout sex," he had said once during our idle chat. "Ya gotta have a mother who know how to teach 'er kids how t' masturbate once they reach puberty, boys or girls!" he laughed. I suppose in that sense he had found the ideal parent for his children.

The swarm of men and women were almost completely naked. They twisted and writhed in wild ecstasy. This was the perfect sexual deviant Shangri-La that I had envisioned. I had been totally defeated by Rokuro Yamazaki. I realized that it took a monster like Mr. Yamazaki to run a place like Deer Park.

I yelped as a hand reached out and clamped onto my arm. I looked down and saw that it was Genjro. He had woken from his drunken nap. His expression was frozen and his eyes were bloodshot as he looked up and said, "Let's go home. The last train is about to leave."

He didn't want to go home, he just wanted to get out of this haunted house. The orgy in the tatami room that was filled with soft limbs that trembled and writhed in sexual pleasure must have looked like a scene of bloody carnage or hell itself—the pale bodies actually ghosts that writhed and cried out in agony, not ecstasy.

I pointed towards the middle of the swirling scene of chaos. Genjiro saw something he absolutely didn't want to see, and sprang back in horror.

Ayako was there, her hair in disarray, her perfect cheeks sucked in as she took Tatsuo's penis deep inside her mouth. Her eyes were closed in a state of intoxicated pleasure as she wandered the line between fantasy and reality. Her body swayed gently, still bound tightly with rope. Ayako kissed his body intently.

"Ah, mother, I think I'm gonna come!" Tatsuo said sorrowfully. He had given over control of his body completely to Ayako's ministrations, and just stood there in front of her.

Ayako pulled her mouth away from his member, and said, "No, not yet. You come too quickly. Let yourself enjoy it a little longer." She kissed his erect penis and his testes. Genjiro stood there in dumb amazement. She felt him watching. Their eyes met, but her expression was indifferent and cool. She was in a dream-like state, having lost her memory of the past entirely. She turned her wet, lustful eyes to Genjiro and said, "Hey, ever since I became a sex slave I've gotten really good at this. Don't leave yet. Stay and watch 'til the very end." Then she opened her lips wide and took Tatsuo's penis deeply into her throat. She ignored Tatsuo's cries, her lips making small sounds as they slipped and sucked his penis.

"Ah, mother, I'm gonna come!" Tatsuo practically screamed. He gripped her sweaty, milk white shoulders as she rocked back and forth furiously. At the moment he climaxed, she pulled away and aimed her flushed cheek towards the head of his penis.

"Aim for it. You can do it, Tatsuo," she said as his hot white semen spurted out and soaked her face.

Ayako's tangled hair clung to her face like tendrils of smoke. She tossed it over her shoulder and turned her steamy gaze towards Genjiro and me.

Her semen-splattered face had such an erotic expression on it that I shivered. It was weirdly beautiful and she fairly dripped with erotic energy.

"Wanna play?" she asked me, a lascivious grin creeping up one side of her face. I shuddered again. For a moment she looked like the fairy queen of the S&M ghost world.

"Well?" she asked again, her voice a sweet whisper. I cursed myself for hesitating. Here I was in the real Deer Park, and yet I insisted on clinging to base human thoughts and emotions. I realized how pathetic I was.

In this hedonistic sect, it didn't matter if Ayako was

Mr. Yamazaki's wife or his sons' lover. She was neither an angel nor a devil; she was just a beautiful, glistening female animal. I finally realized that jealousy and envy had prevented me from getting with this amazing, erotic beast. I felt stupid.

"Are you going to join in?" I turned and asked Genjiro. His face was slack, but his eyes shone with a glimmer of arousal.

"Let's do it like the Yamazaki boys did it. There's nothing to it. Don't think of any of them as people. We're just a bunch of male and female animals."

I took off my necktie. Genjiro, finally persuaded, took of his tie and jacket. He looked like a mental patient suffering from delirium, but he also looked peaceful.

I felt a raunchy smile creep up my face. Ayako moved and twisted her bound body sensually, provoking me. I stripped off my pants as I drew closer to her. By the time I took off my underwear and tossed them away I had a raging hard-on. I felt like I had finally become a full-fledged member of Deer Park. I imitated the Yamazaki brothers when I spoke to Ayako.

"Please, mother..."

Bewitching Bloom
-A Tale of a Porn Star-

IT HAD BEEN SOME TIME since I visited Hakata, in Kyushu. I was invited by an old friend of mine, Mikizo Furukawa, who works in Hakata as a doll maker, to see several dolls he had on display at a traditional art exhibition at a department store on Tenji Nishi Street.

Right after graduating college, Mikizo studied the art of doll-making with master craftsman Kunio Iwasaki. Just twenty years ago he set out on his own, and since then found great success, winning awards at the regional level for technical excellence in doll-making. I met Mikizo when he was studying with Mr. Iwasaki, learning to create molds for dolls. To make a Hakata-style doll, the clay is kneaded, poured into a plaster mold, fired in a kiln to create a porcelain finish, and then the features are hand-painted onto the figure. However, Mikizo had recently been struggling with new challenges facing the art of doll-making. Hakata dolls don't really fit in with modern times and people's lifestyle, so orders for traditional dolls had been on the decline.

Other doll-makers had responded by making dolls that look like celebrity actresses or famous baseball players, hoping to appeal to the modern customer. But Mikizo refused to be corrupted by such influences. He continued to focus solely on creating beautiful, traditional, kimono-clad dolls.

After the exhibition, we headed out to Higashi-Nakasu to have a drink and celebrate. We went to a small restaurant overlooking the Naka river, which reflected the neon glow of the city.

Mikizo talked about the current state of doll-making in Hakata. "After the Bubble burst, everything—education, culture, the arts—had to be reconsidered. The days when I could make whatever type of doll I liked and knew it would sell are long gone. I guess I'm nostalgic for the heyday of Hakata dolls, when my tastes matched the tastes of my clientele, but now I'm older, and the dolls I enjoy making no longer hold any appeal for buyers."

My favorite dolls that Mikizo made were his mounted-bandit Hakata Geisha style dolls, and even when he tried to make a modern-style doll, it would invariably be styled in an *irotomesode,* a single-colored formal kimono or a *kurotomesode*, a black, formal kimono.

Whenever I would write short stories—well, erotic short stories, as usual—that included proper young women in formal kimono dress, I would often base the image on the many Hakata dolls that Mikizo sent me. However, it's very difficult to do justice to the beauty of those kimono with words alone. I would end up calling Mikizo in Kyushu, asking him to explain the designs to me.

"Oh, that's *hitokoshi chirimen* crepe fabric in a single-color kimono style, and the *tsukesage* design is large chrysanthemum flowers." This much I can handle, but another kimono would be in figured satin crepe, patterned with a snowstorm, rolling blue waves and white sand, and at that point I'd be totally confused. Young women's kimono are especially elaborate, for example a long-sleeve kimono made of *koma* crepe patterned in *Higaki*-style, with a drape styled with plum blossoms, citrus *tachibana* blossoms, maple leaves, and camellias. After such long-winded descriptions, I abandoned the hope of trying to depict those impossibly detailed kimono in my stories. It was obvious that Mikizo knew more about kimono cloth and all its styles than the average fabric merchant.

I commented on how nice it must be to make a living painting beautiful doll faces and dressing them to one's own liking. But Mikizo said, "I'm just living in an aesthetic fantasy world. But you, my friend, have spent your career surrounded by living dolls, haven't you? I'm jealous of all the real-life pleasure you've had lavished on you by those women." He was referring to my days spent working at Nikkatsu Roman Porno, and all the porn stars I knew personally way back then.

Nikkatsu Roman Porno was established in 1971 and went dark in 1986, producing films for just fifteen years before disappearing from the face of the earth. It's demise was brought about in part by the managers at Nikkatsu ignoring profitability in favor of expanding business operations, but also by the advent of VCRs and adult videos revolutionizing the pornography business. Adult videos, or AVs, tended to ignore things like "plot" and "character development" and instead focused solely on men and women getting it on. At the farewell party for Roman Porno, the directors laughed bitterly, saying that the demise of their production company was like the forces of evil porn causing the fall of good, high-quality erotic films.

Looking back on the fifteen-year long history of Roman Porno brings back many nostalgic memories. About two years into making films, Roman Porno created an S&M division, based almost exclusively on short stories that I had written. Those films required actresses that could be trained in special skills. The first such actress was Naomi Tani. Naomi starred in fifteen S&M films, and retired in order to marry. The second S&M "queen" was Junko Mabuki, the third was Izumi Shima, and the fourth and final queen was Miki Takakura.

Before the start of Roman Porno, Naomi Tani appeared in various low-budget soft-core "pink films." I wrote the script for many of those films, which featured Naomi in all sorts of bondage, from being simply bound hand and foot to hanging upside-down from the rafters. Of all the S&M queens, Naomi was famous for her physical stamina. In one pink film she played a Meiji-era prisoner, where she was hung upside down and tortured. The scene involved the prisoner's husband, accused of political subterfuge and therefore also tied up for torture. However, the actor playing the husband couldn't handle the extreme physical pain of the bondage. He cried out in pain, and then promptly passed out. Naomi, meanwhile, was totally at ease, literally hanging out, laughing and gossiping with the assistant director between takes. It was at this point that I fully appreciated that women are far stronger than men in the face of physical pain. Mikizo, the doll maker, never met Naomi, but when he came to Tokyo I brought him to the set of Nikkatsu's films and introduced him to Junko Mabuki and Izumi Shima. He later said he had never met such beautiful, well-mannered actresses before. He was so impressed with them that after returning to Kyushu, he sent them each a Hakata doll. The actresses were thrilled, because they thought that Mikizo had created the dolls after themselves, since the dolls' faces somewhat resembled their own.

Compared to porn performers today, the Nikkatsu Roman Porno actresses had a sense of human interest. None of them were in the porn business because they liked getting naked. They all started out pursuing mainstream acting, but failing to break out in show business they ended up in pornography. On top of the shame of failing to make it as a "real" actress, they all secretly carried a slight complex surrounding their involvement in the flesh trade. Because of this, the actresses were easily bedded by the writers and directors. The men would of course defend their actions, saying that if they treated the girls kindly and respectfully, like proper actresses, then they would willingly work in porn. But all that aside, the actresses were renowned for their emotive, expressive acting, and garnered many fans, some of whom would visit the set. No matter how odd or unappealing such fans might be, the actresses never forgot to give them a smile and show their appreciation.

At the time, I was in my forties. I, too, was guilty of seducing newbie actresses.

Seducing Roman Porno actresses was similar to—and as easy as—seducing a geisha. It often went like this: I'd tell the actress that she's caught my attention because her acting had improved recently. I'd mention that her love scenes had become very realistic, very inspiring, and then hint at how nice it would be to experience such pleasure. Then I'd tell her that I'd write a screenplay just for her, implying that if she did me a favor I'd be more than happy to return it. And always, like reading from a script, the girl would reply that she didn't want to be hasty, she wanted to prepare herself, but she'd be in touch in a few days. Like clockwork, the girl would call me a few days later, asking me to take her out the next day somewhere nice. At that point, I'd say, "Sorry, but tomorrow's just no good for me," which would piss her off. "I finally readied myself, and now you're blowing me off? How dare you!" she'd protest. Angry at being jilted, she'd have a fit, call up the director of the current film and take out her sexual aggression on him for a few days. Because of this happy result of our cat-and-mouse-like seduction, the writers and directors often felt like brothers looking out for one another.

Once the line of sexual relations had been crossed, the actresses would use their newfound leverage to press us for more lines and more scenes in which to show off their acting skills. They would get fed up with one sex scene coming after another with nothing of substance in between. They wanted to either have a chance at real acting within Roman Porno films or have the chance to show people that they were legitimately talented actresses. On the occasion that a TV station would call up and ask one of the actresses to appear on a suspense drama or something or other, they'd jump for joy and go all out for the role, no matter how small.

They were all desperate for a chance to shed their porn star image. The actresses who succeeded in achieving legitimate success in mainstream television were Terumi Azuma and Miki Takakura.

One time I invited Mikizo to lunch with several Roman Porno actresses. Afterwards, I asked him which of the actresses he would like to date in real life, if he had the chance. "Izumi Shima," he answered.

Izumi Shima's first hit was *Tokyo Lady Chatterley*. She went on to become a fixture on the S&M scene. She was petite, with a noble and finely chiseled face and a tight, slender figure. She was an accredited traditional Japanese buyou dancer and played the shamisen skillfully, which made her kimono-clad appearance all the more enticing. Her lips would curve into a smile that oozed sex appeal. She was tantalizingly sexy, and any man who saw her wanted to bed her.

In fact, she was excellent in bed. She'd suck, grip and writhe like a woman possessed, and once you'd heard her soft, high cries of ecstasy you'd never forget the sound of it.

Unfortunately she wasn't half as good in love scenes on film as she was in my bed. She'd put on quite a show when we'd make love, and I'd ask her why she couldn't do the same when the cameras were rolling.

"Sex with someone I like is totally different from sex with some actor I barely know," she said. Well, I couldn't argue with her logic.

Izumi Shima excelled in roles that showed off other skills she had, like a sexy voice teacher or something like that.

If Izumi was the epitome of slender sensuality, Junko Mabuki was her opposite—sumptuous, voluptuous and glamorous. Junko was a Sophia Loren type, with an overpowering sexuality that drew rave reviews. Her body was so voluptuous she never wore a kimono in any of her films; they didn't suit her curvaceous figure at all. She looked far more becoming in Western-style evening wear. Junko starred in about ten S&M films for Roman Porno, playing roles like female teachers, nurses, secretaries, even international airline stewardesses. All her sex scenes involved crying while being scolded and reprimanded, but in private, Junko was a wild woman in bed. She was sensual, greedy, aggressive, and could knock a guy off his feet. She wasn't one to dim the lights and hide her sex; she'd sooner have carefree, fun-loving outdoor sex on a sun-drenched sand dune. Men wouldn't be able to hold back against the rough, rhythmic undulation of her hips and they'd come once, twice, and she still wouldn't be satisfied so she'd grab the nearest sex toy and get herself off. She was so energetic and full of vigor that in film scenes where a man who was supposed to be tying her up and torturing her he would end up overwhelmed by her tremendous energy and tortured and worn out himself.

Miki Takakura was a princess type, born into a wealthy

family. She had an air of elegant nobility.

But I should stop; stories about these actresses' sex lives could fill a book. I wrote earlier that these girls needed special training, but in fact I never had to teach them anything. If they thought of it as part of the job, they'd pull off a sex scene without a hint that they secretly hated it. Even if they were in a foul mood or had PMS, they'd let themselves be tied up for a bondage scene without complaint. The staff at Roman Porno suggested posting a wanted ad for willing young women to appear in their S&M films, but I objected. Civilians get excited seeing a beautiful actress tied up and disgraced. If the S&M films featured some plain Jane—no matter how into bondage she was—it wouldn't have the same impact, and wouldn't arouse the viewers as much.

None of Roman Porno's S&M queens, even Naomi Tani, were particularly interested in bondage, and some even grew queasy at the sight of a rope. And yet, at press conferences before screenings they would say they read my stories when they were young and were intrigued by the world of S&M, going on and on brazenly bullshitting their way through the interview. It was that stoic dedication to their work that made me think of those women as real actresses.

Just recently a friend of mine in the adult video industry said he was working on a big-budget porno and wondered if I would be interested in writing the screenplay.

He brought the director and several porn actresses to my house to discuss the film. I started talking about my ideas for a screenplay, but the young director stopped me, saying he wasn't very good with anything dramatic. I was further surprised when one of the actresses said, "I'm not good with lines and stuff. I'm cool with anything sexual. I'll go down on a guy, do all sorts of things in bed, but I can't memorize too many words." And the director was confident when giving instructions during a sex scene but didn't know what to do with a real scripted scene. "So then what do you need a screenwriter for? I don't get it," I said and refused to work on the project then and there. Nowadays erotic and soft-core films are made by this type of staff with that level of actress. I long for the days of Nikkatsu Roman Porno and the actresses who begged for more lines, for more dramatic and challenging roles.

A certain weekly magazine recently ran a six-month-long column featuring interviews with popular porn stars. In the interviews, I was surprised to see the girls wore almost no make up, and were in jeans and a t-shirt, explaining that they came to the interview between gigs. If any Roman Porno actresses had an interview, they'd go all out, spending hours putting on make-up, dressing to the nines in either a kimono or a nice evening gown, doing their best to make themselves as appealing as possible. None of the actresses in the weekly magazine wore a kimono to the interviews. I also knew that none of these girls knew anything about kimono dressing. "You've never worn a girdle, have you," I asked one modern porn actress. "Oh, no, my hair is thick and lovely. I don't need to wear curlers," she replied, completely missing the point.

Every time I find myself lamenting the current trend of emotion-lite porn stars, I reminisce about Nikkatsu

Roman Porno's actresses. Those actresses were sweet and discreet. After a tryst, they'd get all misty eyed and make me pinky-swear promise to keep our affair a secret. A friend of mine still in the industry told me that porn actresses today will gossip with the crew about which directors they've slept with, and had no qualms about outing those that were duds in the sack.

Mikizo the doll-maker said he was nostalgic for the heyday of Hakata dolls; I felt the same nostalgia for the heyday of genuine actresses working in erotic films.

Junko Mabuki, Izumi Shima and Miki Takakura are all married and living a civilian life somewhere out of the limelight. After they retired I haven't heard much of their goings-on. There was a reunion party a few years ago and all the Roman Porno stars were invited, but none attended. They probably didn't want to spoil the image that everyone had of them at the peak of their beauty.

Perhaps they felt that showing the world their aging, tired faces would destroy the mystical image they worked so hard to achieve during their careers. That's why I haven't pushed to keep in touch with any of them.

However, I have kept in touch with the original reigning S&M queen, the celebrated yet feared Bewitching Bloom, the dominant star of the porno world, Naomi Tani. She currently runs several successful businesses in Kyushu. Mikizo had also heard about her successful business ventures. Naomi established a large video-rental store in Fukuoka and is currently looking for other locations to expand the franchise. She also runs a nightclub in

Kumamoto, but the one time Mikizo tried to go, the place was so packed he couldn't get in. But Naomi came out to greet him and he told her that he had been a fan for a very long time. They had their picture taken together to commemorate their meeting.

"Since you're already here in Fukuoka, why don't we go to Naomi's club in Kumamoto?" Mikizo offered.

I went to the opening party for the nightclub about ten years ago, but hadn't seen Naomi since. Out of all the S&M actresses I knew at Roman Porno, I had the strongest, deepest connection with Naomi.

"Good point, my friend. I guess I'll head on over to Kumamoto," I replied.

I called Naomi's club right away.

"Oh, it's so good to hear from you! I'll be waiting for you, so you'd better come!" Naomi's lively voice sang out over the phone. After such a welcoming response, I called up an associate of mine from Shinchosha Publishing, Kusunose, who was also in town covering an event. We were supposed to travel back to Tokyo the next day, but I asked him to stay in town one more night and join me on my trip to see Naomi Tani. Kusunose agreed at once, thrilled at the chance to meet the former queen of Roman Porno.

The next day on the train from Fukuoka to Kumamoto, I asked Kusunose if he knew about Naomi Tani when she was actively performing. He had just turned thirty that year, which means he was still in junior high when Naomi was performing, so he was too young to have seen any of her films in a theatre. He became a fan of hers after discovering VHS copies of the Roman Porno series, and always wanted the chance to meet that voluptuous figure in person. While going through puberty he would get himself off watching Naomi's old films.

"But she's forty-six years old now. I'm sure she's lost all her appeal," he said.

"Well, just wait and see," I told him, chugging my beer.

After arriving in Kumamoto, Kusunose led the way to a fifteen-story luxury New Sky Hotel near the 400-year old Kumamoto Castle. Apparently there was some event going on, because the lobby was packed with foreigners.

Right after checking into my room on the eighth floor I called Naomi's apartment. Our hotel wasn't far from her place; Kusunose had done his homework.

"Okay, I'll meet you at your hotel at six o'clock," she said in her clear, lively voice. She'd been waiting for my call. "We'll stop by my club and then we'll go out to dinner."

Half an hour later she called my room from the service phone in the lobby. I knocked on Kusunose's door, and the two of us headed downstairs.

Kusunose spotted Naomi in the sea of foreigners in the lobby first, and stopped so suddenly I nearly ran into him. There she stood, wearing a kimono, looking as fascinatingly elegant as if she had stepped right out of those Roman Porno films and into the lobby. She was surrounded by several gentlemen, smiling sweetly and chatting gaily. While waiting for us to come downstairs, she ran into one of her regular customers who happened to be there on business. One customer became two, then three, and all of a sudden she was the center of attention, a social butterfly making nice with her customers, even outside the club.

Naomi was wearing a *matsu-kuzushi* style kimono printed with a fine pattern of dew-covered leaves with an *obi* in a pale yellow rose color. It was a fine kimono, befitting a club mistress heading out to work.

It was obvious that Naomi had not just retained her youthful charms, she had blossomed with time. Her sensuality flowed easily from her like a fragrance. Her carriage and manner showed the refinement of someone who was capable of mastering the business of nightlife. Her noble, expressive features, her big, open eyes, the taut bridge of her nose—everything was exactly as it had been twenty years ago. Her jet-black glossy hair was pulled up to reveal her beautiful cheekbones and jaw line. There wasn't a hint of anything that would mark her as middle-aged.

Several foreigners noticed the commotion sur-rounding Naomi and thought that she must be some celebrity, so they took out their cameras and moved in to take a picture.

"Well then, I have to get going. I hope you'll stop by and see me soon," she said and bowed to the gathered crowd of gentlemen, then briskly walked towards Kusunose and me.

"That was the CEO of such-and-such company," she explained as she winded her arm through mine and walked us out of the hotel. She always liked to walk arm-in-arm with people she was close with. When we were younger, we were too shy and awkward to act like lovers, but now she used small gestures like this openly to show her affection.

The valet boy ran up as soon as we were outside.

"Ah, it's been a while, Ms. Naomi. How are you?" he said, flagging down a taxi. A cab pulled up, and the driver stuck his head out of the window saying, "Oh, it's Ms. Naomi!" and immediately got out and opened the door for her.

Naomi had achieved celebrity status in this town.

Once in the cab, I properly introduced Naomi and Kusunose. I had let her know beforehand that he was interested in meeting a porn-star-turned-successful businesswoman.

Naomi had retired at the height of her popularity in 1979 in order to marry, much to the chagrin of her fans. She started up a small nightclub in 1985, but soon after was hit by a motorcycle and was wounded so badly her doctors weren't certain she'd survive. She was bedridden for three years, then divorced her husband, ended up severely depressed for several years, but now here she was running her own business: Naomi Enterprises. She had a talent for business management. Her club is "Otani" (literally "big valley," a pun on both her last name and her generous cleavage), in the Hanabata district of Kumamoto. She had silk lingerie and accessories imported from Europe on display and for sale at the club. In Kasuga, the next town over from Kumamoto, she opened a large-scale video store named Yours, Naomi. The video store carried videos for sale only, not for rental. Revenue from the store broke $100,000 a month.

Naomi said she was thinking about creating original videos. "I want to create an all-inclusive S&M building called Naomi's Castle or something like that. The first floor would be a video store, the second floor would be a rental studio, and the upper floors would have S&M playrooms. S&M is much more mainstream than it used to be. So those playrooms would be a place where men and women could experiment with soft-core bondage. What do you think? I think it would be a hit. I'll get to use all the tricks I learned way back when," she said, tugging on my hand and bursting with excitement as she spoke.

During the day Naomi would pursue her business ventures, but at night she would always return to Otani, dressed up in a fetching outfit that suited her role as a devoted club mistress. She's never missed a day of work at the club. She faithfully keeps the "Naomi Tani" brand alive and cherishes the memories and experiences her career in erotica gave her.

Club Otani is on the third floor of a building right in the middle of Hanabata, the business district of Kumamoto. The club is about 600 square feet, with soft lighting and about twelve hostesses entertaining guests. It wasn't yet eight o'clock, but the booths that lined the club were mostly full. As soon as Naomi entered, everyone cheered.

"Is it always so crowded in here?" I asked Naomi, taken aback by the atmosphere.

"This is nothing. In a couple of hours this place will be jam-packed. Since we're not like a restaurant we can't have people wait for a seat, so we have to apologize to anyone who can't get in and ask them to try again next time. We end up doing that every night," one of the hostesses explained, leading us to a booth near the back of the club.

Naomi brought over several guests and introduced

them to me. I had asked Naomi to introduce us to people she was close with in Kumamoto, and she had asked those people to the club that evening. I had wanted to hear the opinions of her fans and friends in Kumamoto.

Naomi rounded up four gentlemen from around the club and brought them over to our booth. Each introduced himself and handed me a business card. Everyone was a well-known doctor in Kumamoto. Dr. Maeda, the orthopedic surgeon. Dr. Fujimura, the neurologist. Dr. Fukuda, the gynecologist. Dr. Yamamura, the dentist. All these doctors had had their hands on some part of Naomi's body—which is an odd thing to say, but true. Each of them had taken care of her ailments over the years and had become close to her as a result.

After being struck by a motorcycle that sent her flying thirty feet, Naomi lingered on the cusp of life and death. The doctor in charge of her care at that time was Dr. Maeda. During the prolonged divorce trial, Naomi became severely depressed and was treated by Dr. Fujimura.

Dr. Yamamura was the dentist who helped straighten and care for her teeth. At one point Naomi thought she might have uterine cancer, but Dr. Fukuda ran some tests and told her she was all right. Naomi became friendly with each of these doctors, and they often go out drinking or golfing.

The dentist, Dr. Yamamura, started getting tipsy.

"Well, everyone here is very familiar with Naomi's head, or feet, or teeth. But the luckiest has gotta be Dr. Fukuda. The rest of us haven't been able to get between her legs," he laughed. When the dentist asked the gynecologist what she was like down there, he replied, "She's still as sweet and firm as a ripe peach." Everyone laughed, even Naomi.

Every time the door opened and a guest arrived, Naomi would spring to her feet and greet them. Whether it was a CEO or just a random suit, she would indiscriminately pour on her coquettish charms, her feminine instinct clearly at work. The fact that she had the perfect personality to work among civilians as a nightclub mistress honestly came as a bit of a surprise to me, who had known her since she was just a girl.

I met Naomi Tani in 1965, when she was eighteen years old. I had recently quit my job as a junior high teacher at a school on the Miura Peninsula and moved to Tokyo to work at Wako Productions, a subcontractor for a film production company.

My job was to write screenplays for post-production recording, basically adapting the original English script into Japanese that our voice actors could comfortably dub. The titles I remember working on included *The Flintstones*, *The Big Valley*, and *Alfred Hitchcock Presents*. My job as writer meant working closely with the director, going into the recording studio to direct the voice actors through the recording (well really, "looping") process. The director on *The Flintstones* was one Yamaoka, who would later become Naomi's first boyfriend. He's a director now, but he used to be a yakuza thug. He would bring along a group of gangsters and storm into the producer's office at Wako Productions, yelling and demanding he return the money the yakuza had loaned him. The producer, however, was a fairly stubborn man, and ended up turning the tables on Yamaoka. "A young man like you has prospects, a future. Are you sure you really want to throw away your youth running around town, harassing people, doing the yakuza's dirty work?" he asked. "It's not too late, you know. Hey, I have an idea. You could work here with me. I'd be willing to keep you on the straight and narrow," he said persuasively. Yamaoka was dumbfounded, but deeply moved. He decided then and there to wash his hands of the yakuza business. Apparently he was just as easily talked into becoming a gangster as he was talked out of it. The producer said, "I'll make you a director here at Wako Productions. A guy like you could do anything if you just put your mind to it." Yamaoka thrilled to the opportunity, and instantly vowed to reform his ways.

Several other directors at the company were appalled at the idea of a former mobster in their ranks, and voiced their concern to the producer. Ignoring their complaints, he responded by placing Yamaoka in charge of a TV movie.

Of course, none of the writers wanted to have anything to do with Yamaoka. One day, the producer called me into his office, where he introduced me to Yamaoka. "Would you mind working with this young man?" he asked, his eyes betraying his desperation. I'm sure the producer figured a country bumpkin like me would be too dull to put up too much resistance to working with a former gangster.

"I'm just a novice, and would greatly appreciate your assistance on this project," Yamaoka said politely. I began to think I might actually end up liking the guy. At first glance, Yamaoka was sternly handsome, tall and well-built. He was wearing a dark blue fitted suit with several gold rings on his fingers and an expensive silver watch on his wrist, none of which helped dispel the gangster image. I thought to myself that it was unfair and narrow-minded of the other directors to freak out over his appearance.

I invited Yamaoka out to a bar that evening to better get to know him.

"Directing at Wako isn't like directing a film or a play. You're really just giving advice to the voice actors. Any idiot could do it," I told him, feeling a bit tipsy. "I'll be in the booth, working at the mixer, so I'll help you out. Don't worry, it's not hard at all."

We did a test run first, a pre-war black and white C-grade Western. For a proper full-length film, we would gather the actors for a rehearsal before the actual recording, but this type of low-grade movie was usually dubbed in one sitting. However, Yamaoka was either feeling a lot of pressure to do well on his first movie or he simply liked ordering around the voice actors, because he called them in to rehearse two, three times without laying down any recordings. The actors were pissed, of course, made to feel like playthings for this upstart director who insisted rehearsing this C-grade turkey over and over again, so they complained to their manager.

The manager came to talk to Yamaoka, telling him that his actors weren't happy with the way the project was being directed. Yamaoka's eyes widened, his nostrils flared.

"You asshole! I dare you to say that again! I am a well-respected director. A director's orders are just as important as a mob don's!" he suddenly yelled. The poor manager was so shocked he could do nothing but stare back.

The next project we collaborated on was the cartoon *The Flintstones*. Yamaoka, getting a feel for directing, decided against casting professional voice actors, and instead hired Asakusa vaudevillians he made friends with while running around with the yakuza. This made a kind of sense, since *The Flintstones* was a slapstick cartoon based in the prehistoric age. Yamaoka introduced me to a young man he wanted to use in the cartoon. He was a former national flyweight boxing champion, and wanted to break into showbiz. He showed up wearing an ill-fitting gray suit and a bowtie. He was short, with an oblong face which made him look something like Casper the Ghost. His name was Seisaku Saito, and he would later find fame as Hachiro Tako, the comedian. At the time, Hachiro Tako was 25 years old.

Yamaoka explained Tako's current situation. During his boxing days, he was called "Kappa Seisaku" and was famous for being hard to knock down. But apparently he had been knocked around a little too much, and had developed a bit of a speech impediment.

Plus, his memory was dulled quite a bit, so he probably couldn't handle more than a few lines. Yamaoka, even though he was a director, had never bothered to look at the script. If this was an original screenplay then lines could be added or taken away to some extent, but since this was a translation dubbed onto an existing video we didn't have much leeway. No matter how many times I tried to explain this to him he just wouldn't listen. "Can't we do something?"

he'd ask. I tested Tako by having him try and read a little from the script, but it was immediately obvious he couldn't handle even one line. I had an idea, though, that let us use Tako regularly in *The Flintstones*. The catch—he didn't play a human. The Flintstones kept a dinosaur as a pet, and it would howl or groan about three times per episode. I decided this would be a great opportunity for Tako.

"Is this okay?" I asked, and Tako bowed deeply, saying, "I'll do my very best. Thank you very much."

Surprisingly, the fact that this dinosaur role was Hachiro Tako's show business debut isn't very well known.

The first day on the job, Tako had to voice the dinosaur's groan three times, but even then he had a very hard time. He always sounded drunk or drugged, and it didn't sound like an actual animal noise. Tako was embarrassed that he was making so many blunders with such an easy role, and constantly apologized to the other actors in the room. The other actors were moved by Tako's firm dedication to his role, and cheered him on between takes. Finally, when he did a take that made the cut, everyone in the studio burst into applause.

Yamaoka, never one to stay in one place for long, left Wako Productions after finishing *The Flintstones* and set about building a pink film company. At the time a good number of "eroduction" (erotic production) companies were run by former yakuza types. He established Yamaoka Pro, an eroduction company, and asked me to write screenplays for his pink films. I played dumb, saying I specialized in adapting screenplays into Japanese, I didn't know anything about erotica. He wouldn't give it up, though.

"Come on, man. You've got a nasty mind. A dirty mind can write dirty films. Come on, I'm begging," he said.

Yamaoka had a habit of using whatever was handy. The truth was while I was working as a teacher in the countryside, I would sometimes make the students study alone while I wrote erotic short stories that I would later send to a publisher in Tokyo. Yamaoka calling me out as a lecher hardly came as a surprise.

So I gave in and started writing pink film screenplays part-time. The films ended up being hits, and producers from other eroduction companies started requesting my services. The fee for writing a screenplay was about five hundred dollars. My monthly salary from Wako Productions was six hundred dollars, so writing turned out to be a pretty lucrative part-time job. If I averaged two to three scripts a month, then I'd end up making far more from my part time job than my real job. Plus, I only spent about three or four days per script. It was so easy to make bank it was scary.

One day, Yamaoka and one of his former gang underlings, Numata, stopped by Wako Productions. There was a girl who wanted to work in pink films, and they wanted me to check her out. They had her waiting at a coffeehouse in Shibuya, and dragged me out of the office to go and meet her.

Numata drove us to a small coffeehouse in the Dogenzaka district in Shibuya. They wanted me to meet the lead actress for their pink films before writing a screenplay. It was easier to know beforehand what kind of actress would be playing the lead role. The story would change based on her type, if she was voluptuous or if she was slender. At the time I was writing scripts specifically for Keiko Niitaka, Takako Uchida and Yasuko Matsui.

In a corner of the coffeehouse a young girl sat alone, gazing absent-mindedly out the window. When she saw us approaching, she got flustered, standing up and quickly bowing in my direction. I figured she couldn't be older than twenty. Something about her screamed country bumpkin, but she had very nice curves. She wore a white blouse with khaki slacks, and her hair was down. What caught my eye was the way her plump bust filled out her sweater, and how her substantial thighs seemed ready to burst out of her pants. She wasn't wearing any make-up, so it was hard at first to tell if she was really attractive or not. Her face was an odd mix of youthful innocence and ripe maturity melted together. Her lips were thick and sensuous. She was the girl who wanted to get into pink films.

"How old are you?" I asked, pulling up a chair. She batted her eyelashes at me, and replied, "Eighteen."

"I hear you've also picked a stage name. What did you go with?"

She seemed a little nervous when she replied "Naomi Tani," straightening in her seat.

That's a nice name, I said, pulling a cigarette out of its pack. The buxom girl who called herself Naomi Tani flashed a smile, explaining, "I took the 'Tani' from Junichiro Tanizaki, and 'Naomi' is the lead in one of his most famous books. That's how I got 'Naomi Tani,'" she said.

"Wow, you're a fan of Junichiro Tanizaki, huh? What else have you read by him?" I asked, and Naomi's expression stiffened.

"Yeah, uhm, I liked 'Rashomon.'"

"'Rashomon'?"

"Don't bother pushing the issue with this kid," Numata smirked. "She's a drop-out. She thinks Doppo Kunikida's 'Rashomon' was written by Junichiro Tanizaki."

"Doppo Kunikida?" I asked, taken aback by his mistake.

"You idiot. 'Rashomon' is Akira Kurosawa. What the hell is wrong with you morons?" Yamaoka piped in. I wanted to say that he too must have only graduated middle school. Anyways, the people who made pink films back in the day were usually simpletons like this, and I couldn't help but enjoy myself at their expense.

The waitress came to take our orders, and Yamaoka ordered Blue Mountain, Numata ordered Mocha and I went with Kilimanjaro. When asked what she would like to drink, Naomi replied, "I'd like a coffee, please." Everyone couldn't help bursting into laughter.

And that's the story of how I met Naomi Tani, eighteen years old, at a coffeehouse in Dogenzaka, Shibuya. Yamaoka had no idea what he would do with her, but he had a gut feeling that he wanted to keep her under exclusive contract.

There were a fair number of eroduction companies with a stable of exclusive actresses. If an actress showed promise, she would be lent out to other production companies, but would have to give priority to her contract holder. If an actress became wildly popular, her contract holder would refuse to lend her to rival companies, therefore driving up her value. Distribution deals struck with independent pink film production companies were usually based on the popularity of the star and the quality of the writing. The contract fee—in actuality the sale price—would fluctuate based on those factors, but most films generally cost around $18,000 to $20,000.

"We'll start out with a small test. Just write her a small role in your next script," Yamaoka said.

I agreed to the project, and asked Naomi if she was ready to go ahead. She responded in a full-on Kyushu drawl that made Yamaoka and I do a double take.

"Ah am just a country bumpkin, not a year out a' Hakata. Pleased t'make yer acquaintance. All a' my friends made fun of someone like me tryin' to make it in this business, but Ah'll try my best. Ah look forward to workin' wit' you."

This was her attempt to make a good impression on me.

"That accent is rough, my friend. I'll do my best to keep her lines to a minimum," I whispered to Yamaoka.

After meeting Naomi, Yamaoka and I discussed using her in our next pink film in a minor role. A year after leaving Hakata she made her debut in the world of erotic film.

In the coffeehouse in Shibuya, Naomi told us bits and pieces of her personal story. Her parents divorced when she was young, with her father winning custody.

Her father soon remarried, however, and her home life became complicated. Her stepmother then gave birth to a boy, and both parents doted on the new baby and ignored her. During grade school she'd go over to a friend's house right after class. She dreaded dinnertime most of all, when she had to walk alone home. Her father worked as a driver so he was rarely home, and so the house was basically her stepmother's. She was probably teased by her stepmother for being another woman's daughter, which is why she hated going to her house. In middle school, an upperclassman she looked up to like a brother left for Kansai to get a job. Naomi bought a one-way train ticket and followed after him. She somehow managed to work her connections and got a job in Nara working at a confectionery factory, but a teacher from her middle school went after her and brought her back to Hakata. It was apparent even as a young girl that she had wanderlust.

After dropping out of school, she had worked for two, three years, saving up about five thousand dollars. She took her savings and moved to Tokyo. She had no intention of going into show business; she just planned on finding a decent job. Since she was fairly tall she thought she might get work as a model. She started working as a waitress, and one day she was scouted by an agent who complimented her figure and asked if she was interested in working with his modeling agency. The agency, however, turned out to be bogus. Within a month, the agent put on a show, begging in tears, saying he was desperate for a loan. She lent him her hard-earned five thousand, and he instantly absconded with the money. At a loss for what to do and dejected, she started working part-time at a dive bar on the outskirts of town, assisted the popular female ejaculation consultant Michiko Toyohara, and occasionally worked as a model.

In the year since she left Hakata, Naomi led a life similar to that of Marilyn Monroe in her early years. One night Numata was drinking at the dive bar where she worked and asked her if she was interested in taking her clothes off on camera. "And the rest is history," she says.

I started writing a screenplay that would include Naomi as a character, but I couldn't get the sound of her Kyushu drawl out of my head. "Ah can't use that there accent, hun," I thought to myself. So I avoided the problem by keeping her mostly silent, focusing on her appearance instead. I cast her as a young nurse. I forget the title, but the plot was a farce based on the idea of a hospital being a sexual wilderness, with sexually frustrated patients and equally frustrated nurses satisfying each other behind closed doors.

Naomi played a novice nurse, surprised by a patient who grabs her, locks the door and tries to make love to her. To add to the image of a newbie nurse, I let her use her Kyushu accent and yell out, "What tha hell are ya doin'?!" and toss the patient to the ground.

Even in such a hackneyed pink film, it was immediately obvious that Naomi had amazing presence, and the camera loved her.

For her fifth film with Yamaoka Pro, I finally let loose and cast Naomi in the lead. That year, Toei had great success with *Lady Yakuza*, starring Junko Fuji, and I had the idea to use Naomi as a female yakuza. It was perfect, since the original *Lady Yakuza* was also from Kyushu, and so we decided to make a pink film version of the story.

Naomi was an image of dignified sensuality, radiant in a navy blue kimono tied with a Hakata-style *obi*, her jet black hair decorated with a coral comb. She was fascinating and voluptuous, in a way I hadn't seen before. I think the title was *Devil Azami* or something like that. This was the first pink film in years to become a bona fide hit. No one had thought to do a pink film with a female yakuza as the lead, and I honestly don't think anyone but Naomi could have pulled it off.

This film made Naomi a star overnight. It was also the first time I tried using bondage in a film, so *Devil Azami* was the film that started Naomi on her path toward becoming the queen of S&M.

The plot was simplistic: Naomi played a hustler who fled her hometown Izu after causing a ruckus. After working as a vagrant for a few years she returns home to find her former husband, Ginji, now married to the beautiful young Koharu. Ginji was a drunkard who gambled away his money and restaurant, and eventually even his young wife was taken as collateral by the landlord. Naomi and Ginji tussle with their own unresolved drama, and eventually Naomi agrees to go to the landlord and offer herself in exchange for Koharu's release. The landlord takes advantage of the opportunity and forces her to strip naked in front of his henchmen in revenge for Naomi's past betrayals.

As the vagabond Naomi sits casually in the middle of the tatami floor, the evil landlord sneers, "Now, strip off everything you're wearing, with your own hands. I might be kinder to you if you apologize when you're stark naked."

"Then I'll help myself to a cigarette first," Naomi replies, coolly. "I'm ready."

Watching this scene play out, I noted how much her acting had improved. It was deeply satisfying to see her play such a tough-as-nails role.

She wasn't perfect just yet, but she made a serious effort to create the impression of a female yakuza; the way she scowled and boldly laughed in the face of the enemy, the sharpness of her speech, everything came together nicely. Also, even though we told her not to worry about her accent, she did her best to correct her speech. By the time we filmed *Devil Azumi* it was barely noticeable.

The evil landlord tossed a cigarette on the floor near Naomi. She picked it up, and asked for a light from one of the henchmen surrounding her. One of the underlings held out a match, and she said "light it for me," pursing her lips to reach out the unlit tip. The little thug, slightly overwhelmed, sat down and started to light the match. The actor playing the thug was none other than the former flyweight boxing champ, Hachiro Tako. This was his first pink film.

Once the cigarette was lit, Naomi took a long, delicious drag. Tako couldn't help but stare at her. Naomi turned to him and blew her smoke in his face.

"Smoky in here, eh?"

"Yes, ma'am."

"You're funny looking. Like the bastard child of an octopus and a water monster."

"Really?"

"Bring me an ashtray."

"Right away, ma'am."

As Tako got up to fetch an ashtray, one of the older henchmen lost his patience, knocked him to the ground and grabbed Naomi by her obi.

"How long are you gonna make us wait, wench? What, are ya too shy to take off your clothes? Then we'll help you out of 'em!" yelled the thug. Naomi responded by putting out her cigarette on the back of his hand. He yelped in pain and backed away as Naomi stood and coolly surveyed the mob.

"Don't be getting all worked up! You want me to strip, right? Fine, then!" she snapped.

She pulled loose the cord holding her obi in place, and then her Hakata obi unraveled and slipped to the floor. As she removed her kimono and started to loosen the sash holding her under-kimono in place, the camera closed in to focus on her face, her expression a mix of vexation and grim determination.

I loved seeing how each new emotion seeped out and transformed her sensual features like clouds passing over the sun. The girl I had met at a coffeehouse in Shibuya had metamorphosed into a lovely woman. Before, she would braid her hair with ribbons, her girlish features clashing with her curvaceous body. But now she exuded the air of a dignified actress, her melancholic face changed to suit her sensual figure. After her debut, Naomi was rented out to star in about ten other films, and each role revealed a new layer of coquettish sophistication.

As her undergarment slipped off her shoulders and fell

to the ground, she bit her lip in humiliation and covered her bare, plump breasts with her hands. The henchmen, aroused, drew closer, taunting her. "Take off your loincloth!" "Yeah, show us the goods!" "We won't let Ginji's pretty wife go till you're buck naked!" they barked.

Naomi closed her eyes and swallowed her rage as she pulled loose the ties on her charming light blue loincloth.

Hesitation, humiliation, rage, resignation. I don't know of any other pink film actress who could compare to Naomi's ability to give such a finely detailed and convincing performance of an utterly humiliated character. Finally, the last piece of clothing fluttered to the ground, exposing her fine thighs. She hastily covered her privates with her hand and quickly choked back her anger and humiliation as the mob burst into loud laughter. Naomi's face betrayed her chagrin. Naomi portrayed the character's conflict, the façade of a rough-and-tumble gambler crumbling under the pressure of disgrace, crying out in anguish. This total devotion to portraying the process of her character's humiliation was what put her above and beyond any other actress in the business. She was the epitome of the type of woman worshipped by sadistic types like myself.

"Tie this bitch up!" ordered the evil landlord, and Naomi's eyes flashed with panic. They grabbed a rope and pressed in. One man wrenched her hands away from her breasts and from between her thighs and twisted her arms behind her back. Naomi writhed and screamed out, "Damn you! Damn you!" as her hair swung loose over her shoulders. The little thug Tako was in charge of tying her up. He clung to her snow-white naked body from behind and wound the rope through her arms over her arching back muscles. "Should I make a butterfly knot?" he asked. An older thug responded by knocking him upside his head.

Then, Naomi received the ultimate humiliation at the hands of the swarming yakuza. Her ripe, milk-white thighs entwined with theirs, their hips undulating. Her cries, as she writhed in agony to avoid their attack. Her full breasts, pushed up and out by the hemp rope, trembling. This image, to a sadist like me, is as beautiful as any artistic masterpiece.

One evening as I was getting ready to go home, Yamaoka stopped by my office at Wako Productions, asking if we could talk.

We went out to a bar near the office.

Sitting down at the unfinished wood counter, Yamaoka, never much of a drinker himself, kept ordering me decanters of sake.

He waited till I was nicely lit. "You should quit that translating crap. The three of us—you, me and Naomi— should team up and rock the pink film world," he said. It was strange to say that working for a legit film production company was crap and that working in the porn business was better. Yamaoka wanted to contract Naomi and I exclusively, refuse to loan us out to other companies, withdraw from the independent filmmakers alliance and aim for the top. "If I have Naomi as my star and you as my blockbuster writer, Yamaoka Pro will be number one in the industry," he said. He was doing everything he could do to lure me away from Wako. I had been busy with translating there, and had let his orders for pink screenplays fall to the wayside. Simple-minded Yamaoka saw the conflict and tried to bash my day job and make his offer seem attractive. To be honest, I was getting fed up with translating and adapting scripts. After being plugged into a tape recorder all day my ears would ring all night from the onslaught of English. Sometimes I'd jump awake in the middle of the night and see Alfred Hitchcock sitting at the foot of my bed, looking down at me pitifully. Having work-related hallucinations is never a good sign, but I had persevered—my hard work paid off when I was able to move my wife and kids from the countryside to Tokyo. My wife, a middle school English teacher, wanted to be in Tokyo to keep an eye on me, and if I was working an upright job as a translator she was fine, but if she discovered my involvement in the pink film industry she'd throw a fit. I always felt like grotesque erotica was my true calling, and kept telling myself "someday," but now that the opportunity was within reach I was suddenly reticent, and felt the need to retain a bit of decency.

"Naomi says she won't do it unless Mr. Matsujiro's on board, too," Yamaoka said. I used the pen name "Oniroku Dan" when writing erotica, but used the pen name "Matsujiro" when I worked at Wako Productions, so Yamaoka called me "Ma-chan" and Naomi called me "Mr. Matsujiro."

"She loves your writing," Yamaoka continued, "and she loves you, too." As soon as those words left his mouth I felt like my face crumpled up and collapsed. "Naomi says she'd be so relieved if Mr. Matsujiro would continue to write such wonderful scripts for her," he said. I felt like my heart was going to leap out of my chest. I slowly and carefully took a drag off my cigarette.

"So, she really went and said that?" I asked as nonchalantly as possible. I stared up at the ceiling, pretending to be deep in thought. "All right," I said as if I had just made up my mind, and stubbed out my cigarette. "I'll turn in my resignation tomorrow. No, on second thought, I'll turn it in now. I'm sure the boss is still there. Better do it when I'm drunk."

I pulled a piece of stationery out of my briefcase and dashed off a resignation note. Yamaoka was dumbfounded, then thrilled.

"Hey, Ma-chan, a dirty old man like you doesn't belong in some office, hunched over a dictionary, scribbling away," he said, refilling my sake cup. "Whenever you're on set, letting your inner lecher hang out, you look really happy. That's the real Ma-chan, you dirty boy!"

Quit calling me names, I thought to myself, glaring at him sideways while finishing my letter. All at once, I felt like my life had rounded a corner, and I was excited. Everything suddenly turned pink and sparkling before my eyes. A vision of Naomi and all the other pink film actresses floated across my vision. They all turned to me and smiled lovingly.

It took a full week of negotiating with the producer and senior management at Wako Productions before they finally let me go. The shows I was in charge of, *Alfred Hitchcock Presents* and *Strange Stories*, among others, were their highest rated shows, and so they didn't want to lose me. I even fought with one of the managers, a guy named Kuramae. He made a face, and tried to talk me out of it. "I didn't think you were the type to give up a decent job and tool around with a bunch of sexual deviants," he sneered.

"All I'm doing at Wako is rewriting other people's scripts for dubbing. There's no creativity, no dreams here. In the porn industry, I have dreams, a creative outlet, and above all, I have women!" I shot back.

"I've fallen in love with an actress," I told him. "Yes, it's love for love's sake, and I'll follow her wherever she goes. I'm her trusted writer. I'm doing it for love! Do you have a problem with that?" I said, their faces slack as I left them in the dust and dashed out the front door.

I went into a movie theater to cool off and waited until evening before heading to Naomi's apartment in Shinjuku.

Naomi lived in a humble, dreary studio apartment in the Sankou district in Shinjuku. Her window faced a back alley lined with ramshackle dive bars and cheap restaurants with rope curtain entrances. There was a man playing a charamela flute to attract customers to his ramen-noodle cart, and another man taking a piss on a lamppost. It wasn't exactly a charming neighborhood. It may be hard to believe an up-and-coming porn star with several starring roles to her name would live in such a dirty, rundown area, but at the time pink film actresses didn't make that much money. They were paid per day, not per project, so they had to work consistently to make any sort of decent income. Naomi, being in the lead actress category, would earn a daily rate of about three hundred dollars. Each film took about three days to shoot, so all told she was paid a stipend of nine hundred dollars per role. I made five hundred per film, so I had to write at least two scripts a month to be able to pay the bills.

Her place was usually a mess, but tonight Naomi had made an effort to clean up, and everything was tidy and in place. When I told her that I had quit Wako Productions that same day, her face lit up with a bright smile. She raised both arms and cried, "Banzai!"

"I'll run out and get us something to toast with. Wait here, I'll be right back," she said, grabbing her shopping bag and slipping on a pair of red thong *geta* sandals before heading out the door.

I pulled the ashtray closer and sat down in the middle of her tiny apartment to have a smoke. She had a small sitting desk, apparently bought from a thrift store, that she had polished up nicely and decorated with a light blue vase with a single red artificial flower inside. Next to the vase was a pink film screenplay she was working on. Posters featuring Naomi in films by Rokuho and Million Productions were casually tacked to the walls. And on one of the walls was a black men's jacket.

I recognized the jacket immediately—it was Yamaoka's. I remembered seeing him on set wearing the exact same jacket. On a hanger next to the jacket was a plaid suit that was most definitely Yamaoka's as well. As soon as I realized that, I felt all the blood drain from my face. Once I figured out that they were sleeping together the room suddenly seemed uncomfortably small. "Damn, so that's what's been going on," I moaned, feeling like the wind had been knocked out of me.

Neon light flickered through the soot-covered window and illuminated Yamaoka's black jacket. I stared at the jacket despondently, as Naomi's *geta* covered feet clacked towards the door.

"Does Yamaoka spend the night here?" I asked with my back still turned to her.

"Yes, he does," she answered openly, without a hint of irony, and without a clue that anything was amiss. She didn't realize that my deflated expression was caused by my jealousy over their relationship. Suddenly, I was angry, and headed to the bathroom to try and calm myself down. On the way I stepped on something sharp and cried out in pain. A necktie pin on the floor had attacked my foot. I yanked it out as Naomi said, "Oh, that must be Yamaoka's pin. I guess he left it here by mistake." She gave an embarrassed giggle as I threw the pin at her angrily. She caught the pin effortlessly with one hand and quietly slipped it into her apron pocket.

"I actually wanted to talk with you about that. Would you mind, Mr. Matsujiro?" she asked, placing single serving Ozeki sake cans on the dining table.

The conversation only plunged me further into despair.

"I'm so totally in love with Yamaoka. The nights he doesn't come over I'm so lonely I can't even sleep. Are all women this helpless when they fall in love? What should I do?" she asked. It was all so stupid I could barely listen with a straight face. Apparently they had been together for just over a month at that point.

That bastard didn't even have the decency to tell me he was sleeping with Naomi, I thought bitterly, washing down my sorrows with the cheap Ozeki sake. I suddenly remembered a little while back when we had gone out drinking he had seemed oddly worn out. When I asked him what was up, he said that he had been up all night screwing a woman who was madly in love with him. She kept at him and wouldn't let him get a minute's rest. I realized that that woman must have been Naomi. When I had enough to drink and felt bold enough to mention that story to her, Naomi, being the way she is, giggled "Yeah, Yamaoka's amazing. He didn't let me get a wink of sleep that night."

"So, with both of us under exclusive contract with Yamaoka Pro, he'll be three times as strong. Let's do our best to make a real man out of him," she said, reaching out her hand to shake on our supposed deal.

The idea of helping Naomi try to make a man out of Yamaoka suddenly made me feel like I was lost at sea. I had left Wako Productions and entered the porn business full time on the premise that Naomi was mine to pursue. But now that Naomi had been taken by Yamaoka, I felt like I had lost my only reason for taking the plunge, and was at a bit of a loss for what to do. I let my unrequited feelings and jealousy get the better of me.

"Are you really okay with being Yamaoka's girl? He used to be a yakuza, you know. And he's got a reputation for being a lady-killer." With each rumor I let fly, I felt my self-loathing well up for badmouthing my friend. Naomi didn't seem to be surprised by any of it.

She puffed up proudly, saying, "I know it's a typical trap for women to fall into, but I'm sure that I'll be the one to get him cleaned up and turned around." What pissed me off more than anything was that I wanted to yell from the rooftops that I was the one that loved her. She was totally clueless about my feelings.

In the two years after quitting my job at Wako Productions my life completely changed. In standing up against the tide of the status quo and pursuing my dreams, my efforts finally started to bear fruit. We formed "Tako's Troupe" around Hachiro Tako, sending them on tour at movie theaters around the country; used several pink film actresses in a book of bondage photography; and ran a serialized version of the shots in a monthly magazine run by Haga Publishing in Kanda. With the success from the monthly publication, I rented an office in Shibuya, established the magazine *S&M King*, and created Oni Productions. I bought a 4,500-square-foot house in Meguro, with a garden and a small pond.

I would never have thought things would go so swimmingly well just two years after entering the world of erotica full time. I had always known that pornography was my true calling, but I had to credit Yamaoka and Naomi for giving me the shove I needed. Yamaoka set up "Naomi and Friends," sending her on tour as well. I was also keeping busy with Yamaoka Pro, writing screenplays for Naomi to star in. It wasn't like I was intentionally getting back at Naomi for "dumping" me, but I always ended up writing stories that ended up with Naomi in bondage.

Yamaoka begged me to tone down the abuse, but I ignored him. Each film was a hit, so he couldn't really complain. However, the pink film industry had entered its twilight days. It was 1968, the year that Nikkatsu established its Roman Porno film division. Nikkatsu's mainstream films had been losing money, and so they set their sights on the pink film industry, which raked in about $45 million per year. Nikkatsu held a board meeting and decided to launch an erotic film division, hoping to capture at least half the market share. The effect on smaller independent eroductions was instantaneous, and many had no choice but to shut down operations. As soon as Nikkatsu Roman Porno was established, Yamaoka Pro closed its doors.

After a regional tour, Naomi and Yamaoka stopped by my house in Meguro with souvenirs in hand. They seemed to be on excellent terms.

They would sometimes bring along other troupe members, all of whom—men and women alike—adored and respected Naomi. When I asked one of them what attributes he liked, he said he was impressed by Naomi's passion and determination and her down-to-earth attitude, and the way she liked looking after others. I added that she was appealing because she didn't fall in love easily, but when she did it didn't matter what type of guy it was, she would become totally and hopelessly attached. I also figured that her lack of common sense and her ignorance as a result of dropping out of school made her seem more innocent and accessible.

The main reason Naomi stopped by my house after

coming home from her tour was to retrieve a black leather bag she had left in my care. The bag contained about five or six thousand dollars in large bills. She was too nervous to travel with so much cash, so she wanted to leave it with me. When I asked why she didn't just take the money to the bank, she replied, "But I don't know anyone at the bank. They're all strangers."

This was typical of her way of thinking. Not that I minded being entrusted with all that money. I would occasionally help myself to an interest-free loan.

On the subject of lacking common sense, I myself made an embarrassing blunder while working on a bondage photography book. I had been writing essays for a weekly magazine, and the illustrator Akira Uno had worked with me, creating drawings to accompany the articles. One day as we were heading home after a night of drinking in Roppongi, he said, "There's a cameraman I know who's interested in working on your bondage book. I think you should meet with him."

"What's his name?" I asked.

"Kishin Shinoyama," he replied.

"Is he any good?"

"He's been pretty busy lately, so I'm sure he'll be fine."

Akira probably figured out during this brief exchange that I had no idea who Kishin Shinoyama was, and one would think that he'd call me out of my ignorance. There are, however, quite a few artists who only know how to play dumb in that kind of situation. To make matters worse, I said, "There have been a lot of hacks trying to pass themselves off as photographers recently. I'll do a test shoot with him first."

"Really? A test, huh?" Akira blinked, mystified.

"I'll be at the office tomorrow," I said, getting into a cab. "Tell that Kishi-whatever his name is to bring a few recent nude shots to my office for an interview."

"Ah, right," Akira replied, dumbfounded.

The next day the famous photographer casually dropped by my office.

He had frizzy, reddish brown hair that fanned out about his round face. He wore a leather jacket and jeans which made him look like a bike gang leader. He carried an envelope containing the photos I had requested.

"I heard that you wanted to see my work," he said, laying out his photos on my desk. What happened next was so horrible, no matter how much time passes I still burn with embarrassment just thinking about it. I picked on this internationally renowned photographer's work.

"This angle isn't very good. You should have added more light in this one," I said, acting like a big shot even though I wouldn't know a lens or a filter if it hit me on the head, and the photographers we had worked with before were all amateurs who had taken a couple of photography classes in school.

Kishin listened intently to my bizarre lecture, folding his arms and saying, "Ah, I see what you mean. Yes, indeed."

This idiot has no clue who I am, he was probably thinking. But he played along, pretending to care what I said about his work. He didn't act like a big shot at all;

in fact, he lightened the mood by joking and laughing out loud. I thought he had a great personality, and liked him immediately. I asked him to come back the next day and meet with the publisher to discuss the details of the project. As soon as he left, I called the publisher at Haga. "There's a newbie photographer I want to use for the next bondage photo book. I saw some of his work, and some of it's a little rough around the edges, but I think he has real potential. His name's Kishin Shinoyama, and he's a real kick in the pants."

The publisher laughed when I mentioned his name. "Wow, kids these days have no shame. That guy has real balls, passing himself off as Kishin Shinoyama to try and make a deal."

I described the photographer's appearance to the publisher. "His hair was ratty, like a bird's nest, and he wore a leather jacket and jeans."

"You moron! That's the real Kishin Shinoyama!" the publisher yelled hysterically.

"You mean he's famous?" I said, shaken.

"How do you not know who Mr. Shinoyama is?" the publisher scolded. "He's a globally renowned A-list photographer. He has a huge spread of a Rio Carnival in this month's *Playboy*. Do yourself a favor and go buy it. And you called him a newbie you wanted to try out. Ha! You've got some nerve," he rattled on before hanging up and heading over to my office. I couldn't just wait idly for him to show up, so I dug out Kishin's business card and called his office.

"I know they say ignorance is bliss, but I'm so

embarrassed that I didn't know you were such a famous photographer. I feel like I just preached at Buddha himself," I apologized.

Kishin just laughed. "Well, I just thought you would have figured it out if we worked together," he said in his happy-go-lucky way.

A few days later we met with the publisher. A team was formed with Kishin Shinoyama as photographer, Akira Uno working on layout and me working as general editor.

We booked a number of models and started shooting *The Bondage Encyclopedia.*

To make this a deluxe edition, I wanted to use Naomi as our top model. She was on tour with "Naomi and Friends," and so I couldn't get a hold of her. I got in touch with a member of the troupe, who told me that she and Yamaoka were due to return to Tokyo by the end of the month.

However, when I tried calling Naomi's apartment at the end of the month she still wasn't home. A week passed and still no word from either Naomi or Yamaoka, despite the fact that they always called me as soon as she was back in town. I had no idea what had happened to them. Kishin's bondage photo shoots were running along on schedule, and I was worried that at this rate, the project would end without Naomi's participation.

Eventually the project wrapped, and Naomi wasn't included in *The Bondage Encyclopedia.* I regret to this day the fact that Kishin Shinoyama never got the chance to shoot Naomi in bondage at the peak of her womanhood. I'm sure it would have been a masterpiece.

I found out that Naomi couldn't be tied up because

she was being held up by the police.

One day when I was busy working on *The Bondage Encyclopedia* a couple of cops came to my office. I was shocked when they told me that Yamaoka and Naomi were being detained on the charge of violating child welfare laws.

They had hired a sixteen-year-old girl to work—nude, of course—in "Naomi and Friends" and a detective from the juvenile crime division had them arrested.

One of the detectives placed a photo in front of me, asking, "Have you ever seen this girl?"

I had indeed seen her. Naomi had introduced her to me as a member of her troupe. Her name was Keiko. She had wide-set eyes and was fairly tall, so no one who saw her would ever think she was only sixteen. Any number of pink film actresses lied about their age on their resumes, and apparently Keiko had lied when she said she was eighteen, although I wouldn't have given it a second thought if she had said she was twenty. Since Naomi thought she was eighteen she brought her into the troupe, but Keiko turned out to be a bad seed. She stole some of Naomi's jewelry and ran away from "Naomi and Friends." The police detained Keiko, but when Naomi and Yamaoka went to file a police report for the stolen goods, they discovered that they had hired a minor to work in a nude show and arrested them instead. It was a bizarre situation, with the thief freed and the victim imprisoned.

"Have you used this girl in any of your photography collections or magazines?" the cop asked. Yamaoka had, in fact, asked me to use Keiko in a bondage photo shoot, but

I was too busy to bother with being arrested in violation of child welfare laws.

"No, we haven't used her," I replied.

"Oh, okay," he said, and didn't press any further.

I thanked the heavens that these were fairly stupid cops. I served them tea and they relaxed and we chatted.

The older of the two cops said, "During this investigation I've really come to appreciate what a good woman Naomi is. Right? Great tits, great ass—curves that were made for sex. She's the greatest porn star ever." The younger cop piped in, "Oh, but don't worry, we won't be strip searching her," flushing with embarrassment.

"What's really amazing is how she covers up for her man," he continued. "She wrote in her statement that she was the one who met Keiko and hired her without checking her real age. She said Yamaoka was against hiring Keiko. She insists that Yamaoka had nothing to do with this incident. But the more we investigate, the more it seems like the exact opposite is the truth. Any man would be lucky to have a wife like Naomi."

I used this chance to plead for Naomi's release.

"I'm about to start work on a major project, and would be most obliged if you would be lenient in this case and release Naomi. I can vouch for her as her guarantor. In exchange, I wouldn't mind at all if you kept Yamaoka as long as you need for questioning."

Naomi was released five days later. The cops called my office, and I had my driver Tsumura pick her up from the police station and drive her to my house in Meguro.

It was her first experience being jailed, and the stress had left her emaciated. When I asked if there was something in particular she was hungry for, she said "sushi" without even thinking. I took her right away to a sushi restaurant in Gonnosuke-saka.

That sushi was the best she'd tasted her whole life. She'd repeat that phrase often over the years. "It's kind of like the way your first meal of sushi is amazing after a long trip overseas. But the taste of good sushi after a week in a police cell tastes twice as amazing as that," she'd say. Even after our meal with Kusunose at a high-end restaurant in Kumamoto, she laughed and insisted that that sushi she had after being locked up was the best meal she'd ever had.

As she tucked into her sushi dinner with gusto at that restaurant in Meguro, her eyes filled with tears. "I feel so bad that I'm sitting here eating this amazing sushi while Yamaoka's still sitting in jail," she whimpered. He was finally released about five days later.

Naomi was seriously depressed at the time. Yamaoka Pro had gone belly up, which in turn had forced "Naomi and Friends" to suspend operations indefinitely. I was her main employer, using her occasionally as a bondage model in my *S&M King* magazine. Yamaoka was probably depressed as well, but instead of sitting around worrying he set about starting up a talent agency.

And then, suddenly, an opportunity arose for Naomi to blossom again on the silver screen. As always, just as her luck seemed to only get worse, things would suddenly change for the better. If you were to graph the story of her life, it would show a zig-zag line.

One day several producers from Nikkatsu came to my house in Meguro to work out the details of their new S&M division of films. They brought with them several of my books that featured S&M and bondage. They wanted to produce bondage films based on my erotica. They planned on installing an actress to star in those films. The producers had already decided which actress they would use: Naomi Tani.

"We've seen Ms. Tani's work in pink films, many of which you wrote the screenplay for. I have to ask, is she actually a masochist?" asked one of the producers.

"No, she doesn't particularly have a masochistic personality, but something about her draws out a sadistic side in men—myself included. I always find myself writing scripts that end up with her tied up, and really enjoying it," I explained.

We decided the first film for Nikkatsu's S&M division would be based on a story of mine that had been serialized and published as a novel called *Flowers and Snakes*. We started filming in the fall of 1973. Two veterans of Nikkatsu, Masaru Konuma and Yozo Tanaka, worked on the film as director and screenwriter, respectively. Naomi nailed the role. The film was a huge hit. The *Wife* trilogy followed, with *Sacrificial Wife*, *Lady Moonflower*, and *Lady Black Rose*, all of which were hits. The name "Naomi Tani" became synonymous with S&M. The Nikkatsu Roman Porno films' production budgets averaged around $300,000, so the scale of production was fundamentally grander than independent pink films which were usually made on just

$20,000. Naomi took to the films like a fish to water, finally able to flex her abilities again. I was busy writing a monthly serialization of a five hundred page S&M novel. I noticed that the heroines in my stories began to resemble Naomi. As soon as the serial version ended it was released as a paperback, then the book was adapted for Nikkatsu Roman Porno as a film for Naomi to star in, and then the cycle repeated. I had her in mind while writing a whole range of characters, from the wife of a conglomerate's powerful leader in *Caged Fairy* to a man-eating spitfire lady yakuza in *O-Ryu's Passion*. Naomi Tani was the queen of Nikkatsu's S&M films, and some went so far as to call her the savior of Nikkatsu. Without her, they probably would have gone bankrupt.

During that time Yamaoka started acting suspiciously. He was working on building up his talent agency, and one day he introduced me to a girl he wanted to break into showbiz. She was very lovely, but still just a high school student. When I asked where they had met, Yamaoka said while he was locked up on charges of violating child welfare laws, he met a guy that knew a girl in his neighborhood that wanted to become an actress. As soon as he was out of jail, he introduced them.

"She'll be graduating soon," Yamaoka said. "When she does, I want her to work as Naomi's assistant and get some on-the-job training. I've already thought up a stage name for her," he said, grabbing a pen and scribbling a name on a piece of paper. Terumi Azuma, it read. She was eighteen.

"Pleased to meet you," she said, and quickly bowed her head. Her eyes were dark, but wide and expressive. She was charming and attractive. I remembered that Naomi was just eighteen when I met her and she greeted me in that thick Kyushu accent. Looking at this young Terumi sitting beside Yamaoka, I wondered if there was trouble ahead. Naomi no longer worked with Yamaoka since his production company folded. She was Nikkatsu's cash cow, becoming more and more independent. This new development probably left him feeling very conflicted and agitated. Yamaoka wasn't much of a drinker, so it didn't take a huge stretch of the imagination to think that he would distract himself with a new girl.

One night a few months later, Yamaoka and Naomi stopped by my house unexpectedly. It was out of character for them.

"I brought Kiyoshi Atsumi along," Yamaoka said, waving him over to the entryway. "We've been friends since my days with the yakuza."

I don't know if Kiyoshi was a delinquent in his younger years, but he was famous for his *Mr. Tora* film series. I was flustered by the fact that this famous actor was suddenly at my house.

"My agency is nearby, in Daikanyama. I was hanging out with Yamaoka and Naomi, and they said that a writer friend of theirs lived in a haunted house in Meguro. I thought I'd stop by and see if I could meet any ghosts," Kiyoshi said. Rumor had spread that my house was haunted. My family got so freaked out they moved into an apartment nearby, and I was currently the only one who lived there. Honestly, I was happier living alone—I could concentrate on my writing. But Yamaoka and Naomi always commented on how impressed they were by the fact that I could live with ghosts. They were more spooked than I was. They had both "seen" ghosts in the house, and Naomi started telling people exaggerated stories about my house. It got so bad that one day a camera crew from a local TV station came to do a story on the writer who lived in a haunted house. Thing is, even though I lived there, I never once saw a ghost. But I couldn't help but wonder if something was there, since both Naomi and Yamaoka reported seeing the same type of ghost. I had wanted to get an expert's opinion on the place.

"I have a bit of an interest in ghosts myself," Kiyoshi said, sitting down on the tatami floor.

"Ah, this is for you. Just a small token," he said, pulling a bottle fo Napoleon brandy from his gray jacket. It was late autumn and the wind was cold, but Kiyoshi wanted to leave the glass back door open to the garden out back where the paper lanterns around the pond were all lit. We wanted to hear about Kiyoshi's adventures traveling around while filming, and thanks to his vaudeville comedian streak we all ended up in stitches. Naomi and Yamaoka were laughing too hard to even think about being scared. Kiyoshi apparently took a liking to my garden. He would occasionally pause in his storytelling and gaze out at the lanterns giving a soft glow to the garden. "Doesn't seem like the ghosts want to come out to play yet," he said.

After that night, Naomi would bring Kiyoshi over to my house at least once a month.

Before one such visit, Kiyoshi called and asked me to call over a bunch of people from the neighborhood to scare away the ghost. "We'll make so much noise we'll turn your gloomy haunted house into a happy ghost-free house!" Kiyoshi declared. Danshi Tatekawa, Sanshi Katsura and other performers often stopped by, but Kiyoshi was the only one to suggest having a party to scare away ghosts.

So I called around to the local sushi and soba restaurants, to the liquor store, the grocery store and even the little shop that sold altar equipment and told everyone to come to my house that night, and that Kiyoshi Atsumi was the guest of honor.

As soon as everyone heard that Mr. Tora, the famous heartbroken tramp from Shochiku's *It's Hard Being a Man* series would be there, people who usually crossed the street to avoid walking past my supposedly haunted house thrilled to the occasion and rushed over. Kiyoshi had said he wanted everyone to make a ruckus and scare away the ghosts, but in reality he just wanted to sit and talk with ordinary people about their daily lives.

"Okay, old man, you sit there. And you, dear lady, sit over here. And you my pretty girl, don't be shy, sit here, closer to me. And you, young man, there's room for you out on the porch. Now, what will we talk about? Oh, I know. Miss Naomi, tell us about the difficult work you did in the pink film industry. I'm sure you had a rough time," Kiyoshi said without any hint of pretension. You would never know he was the famous Mr. Tora.

Even though I didn't ask for anything, the sushi restaurant had a boy bring over large platters of sushi, and the liqour store owner brought over several bottles of sake and canned sardines. I guess they felt bad showing up to hang out with a famous actor empty handed. Other people in the neighborhood that I'd never met before caught wind of the impromptu party and carried in baskets of fruit and snacks. Some housewives even brought along their kids and gave them special paper to get an autograph from Kiyoshi.

He obliged everyone's requests to tell funny stories and gossip about his work on the Mr. Tora series, but he was more intersted in hearing about normal people and their day-to-day lives. He liked hearing about the hard work done by sushi chefs, soba noodle makers, even delivery boys. Kiyoshi was an excellent listener, and would nod along, saying "I see. Yes, I understand," and then interject with a funny story on the same topic that would have everyone in stitches. I assume this kind of back and forth with regular folk was incredibly useful to his work as an actor.

I'm sure he cherished his showbusiness friends as well, but seeing him in such a good mood when surrounded by people he didn't know made it seem like he was always seeking out a particular brand of isolated loneliness. It came out in his style of comedy. It was that sadness that made his Mr. Tora character seem closest to his own personality.

When asked how he met Yamaoka, Kiyoshi poked two fingers into my back several times.

"Hurts a little, doesn't it? Gets you a little pissed off the first time it happens, right?" he said, laughing.

Apparently this is what young punks would do to vaudeville actors in bars in Asakusa.

"Yamaoka poked me, and glowered at me like this," he said, narrowing his eyes, which suddenly gleamed with a hint of something dangerous. If this was an accurate depiction of Yamaoka in his yakuza days, then he was one scary kid. Anyways, this is how they met, and the two became close friends. People meet under the strangest circumstances.

At that time I would often hold photo shoots during the day for my magazine *S&M King* at my house. After hearing this, Kiyoshi brought along his friend Keiroku Seki to watch and learn. The set-up featured the model suspended by a rope from a rafter, and Keiroku lended a hand to the staff, hoisting up the model. Kiyoshi, on the other hand, tucked himself into a corner of the room. He was stunned. He would look up at the ceiling, then suddenly avert his eyes. He fidgeted, munching incessantly on crackers. Once the model was released from the bondage and her feet were back safely on the floor, Kiyoshi rushed up to her, saying, "Good work. That must have been very tough," and pressed a cracker into her hand.

Naomi and Yamaoka's relationship started to fall apart in the end of 1978. The beginning of the end was Yamaoka's affair with another woman. Just as I had feared, the woman he was sleeping with was none other than Terumi Azuma.

Terumi first worked as Naomi's assistant, and occasionally appeared in Nikkatsu's S&M films in small roles. Naomi spoiled Terumi, treating her like a teacher's pet, and Terumi followed Naomi around like a puppy, calling her "big sister." Even with their apparent mutual affection, Naomi took pains to teach Terumi the strict manners and etiquette of a professional actress. She taught her how to appropriately attend to the director and how to treat the crew on set. However, one time Yamaoka was on location for their film and showed special interest in Terumi. This obviously put Naomi in a foul mood, and she made no attempt to hide it. The director of the film wanted Terumi to be completely naked for a love scene, but Yamaoka flatly refused to let that happen. "Terumi might cross over into TV soon, and I don't want that kind of nude scene to ruin her reputation. Anything but full nudity," Yamaoka ordered.

Yamaoka was busily working his connections, trying to get a foot in the door for Terumi's big mainstream break. Terumi was sharp and a fast learner, and she was growing more beautiful by the day. I also felt it would be a waste to let her talents grow and fade within the porno industry alone. Naomi was uncomfortable with Yamaoka's preferential treatment of Terumi.

"We're working for Roman Porno. If you're so worried about her getting naked then you should introduce her to a legit talent agency and have done with the porn industry," Naomi said.

"Terumi's not like other porn actresses. She has real talent. I'm having her work in Roman Porno films so she can learn acting. It's for her own good that I'm not letting her strip. It's enough to have you doing all the naked stuff," Yamaoka countered.

The worst part was that Naomi and Yamaoka would

have these arguments and then come over to my house to finish the fight. It was their worst trait, almost like they needed a referee for their quarrels. One day Naomi got very worked up and called my house. The first thing out of her mouth was "Yamaoka has been sleeping with Terumi and you've been keeping it from me, haven't you." I hadn't exactly kept anything from her, but Yamaoka had ordered me to keep my mouth shut.

"I don't know what you're talking about," I bluffed.

"I won't tell him that I heard it from you," Naomi pleaded. "I just want to know the truth."

Well, it's bound to come out at some point, I figured. "Don't tell Yamaoka that I was the one who told you," I said, then told her everything. While Naomi was away touring, Terumi and Yamaoka visited a hot spring spa together, and when they came back they brought sweet dumplings from the spa as a souvenir. They made it painfully obvious that they were having an affair. As I was blurting out everything Naomi suddenly gave a loud wail that stopped me cold. Then just as suddenly she said in a calm whisper, "thank you," and hung up the phone. Not five minutes passed when a high-strung Yamaoka called.

"You're such an asshole. Why did you have to go and tell Naomi everything? Traitor! I'm so pissed off!" Yamaoka yelled, then suddenly hung up. What had happened? I told Naomi not to say she heard it from me. And yet within five minutes she went and told Yamaoka what had happened. What a woman, I thought. But then I found out that they had been fighting in the same room when Naomi first called. "I've never laid a hand on Terumi. If you don't believe me call Ma-chan!" Yamaoka had said, so she called me and I told her the truth. I couldn't blame Yamaoka for feeling like I betrayed his friendship.

The next year, 1979, Naomi Tani ended up announcing her plans to retire. We ended up collaborating on a total of fifteen Nikkatsu Roman S&M films.

The producer Koji Okamura came to me to discuss plans for Naomi's farewell project. I thought the best role to showcase Naomi would be a female prisoner. I recommended *Rope Hell*, published by Sanseisha. The title was changed to *Rope and Skin* for the film version. The director was Shogoro Nishimura of Nikkatsu, the screenplay was written by Isao Takagi, and the supporting cast included Junko Miyashita, Yukiko Tachibana and Shohei Yamamoto.

A popular sports magazine ran a full-page ad: "Reigning queen of the S&M world Naomi Tani to retire after next film! Will she be able to endure her final torture?"

I ended up so involved with the film that I was practically Mr. Nishimura's assistant director. That may have been part of the reason that this film stands out from Naomi's other Roman Porno films in my memory. Naomi played a yakuza card dealer, and her voluptuousness and her gruesome torture scene made her final film a masterpiece.

"I'm going home to Kyushu to get married," Naomi announced to me the month after the release of her last film. We were in the dressing room of the burlesque theatre Nichigeki Music Hall, where Naomi performed her farewell show.

At the time the Nichigeki Music Hall would feature

popular porn stars each month in their strip shows. I had worked on shows with actresses like Kyoko Aizome and Izumi Shima, but of course the farewell show for Naomi Tani, the Queen of S&M, was sold out from day one.

Naomi went through a rough period dealing with the love triangle, but in the end she ended up letting go of Yamaoka and letting her beloved assistant have her man to herself. Naomi looked thoroughly relieved to be done with the relationship. But I was surprised that not even a year later she was planning on getting married.

"Aren't you just getting married to get back at Yamaoka?" I asked, but Naomi shook her head, saying, "No, that's not it, that's not it at all. He's from Kumamoto, right near my hometown of Fukuoka. He's been a fan of mine since as long as I can remember. Last year he proposed to me."

"What does he do for a living?" I asked.

"He wanted to become a professional enka singer, which is why he's here in Tokyo. But to be honest he really doesn't have much of a chance of getting ahead. So he's moving back to Kyushu, and he's determined to bring me back with him. He wants us to have a proper wedding there," she said. It didn't sit well with me.

"Sure, I understand that he's a failure and that's why he's going home to Kyushu, but I don't see why he has to force you to retire at the height of your popularity. Sounds like he's a typical jealous man who can't stomach his woman being more successful than himself," I opined, and again she shook her head, saying, "That's not it. This is love. I spent a rough nine years as Yamaoka's girlfriend, but Mr.

Obayashi is different. He's not that kind of man. I'm sure he'll make me very happy."

She had just broken off her relationship with Yamaoka after much fuss, and I was impressed with how quickly she recovered. She was head over heels in love with Yamaoka for nine long years, but as soon as she realized that it was better to give up on him she made a totally clean break. She even seemed a little coldhearted afterwards.

"Hey, can you bring Mr. Obayashi here?" she asked a petite young assistant. Obayashi was in the theatre to see Naomi's farewell performance.

The assistant led Obayashi to the dressing room. Just as Naomi had told me he was fairly tall and had a handsome leading-man type of face. He was a man of few words, but he kept repeating his promise to make Naomi a happy woman. Naomi looked very happy as she stood next to him and took his hand. She struck a pose and sweetly asked me to take a picture of the happy couple.

Naomi's farewell show at the Nichigeki Music Hall created quite a stir. The story was adapted from the famous Shinnai ballad "Raven at Dawn." We didn't use any Western music at all, only a shamisen. It was a style of performance that hadn't been seen at the Music Hall until that point. I cast her in the role of the courtesan Urazato. It was the best type of role to showcase her acting talent. A typical porn actress would have a hard time playing such a role assisted with just a shamisen, but Naomi fleshed out the character perfectly. This was the final project we worked together on after many years as collaborators.

The curtain rose on a courtyard of a geisha house.

Snow lay thickly on the roof and pine trees. Two shamisen plucked out an overture to the tune of "Raven at Dawn" as Naomi made her entrance dressed as Urazato.

"Naomi, we missed you!" "Please don't retire!" shouted people from the packed audience. Urazato ran away from the geisha house to pursue the man of her dreams. But her master Gyutaro captured her and tied her up, with Urazato wearing just an under-kimono beneath the ropes. He dragged her along the passage through the audience to the stage to the courtyard where she would be punished for running away. Urazato's kimono was open at the collar and the hem was ragged from running through the streets. Even as she was dragged back to the house, exhausted and unsteady on her feet, she kept looking back forlornly over her shoulder to where her lover had been waiting.

"Hey, give it up already, you whore!" Gyujiro said, slapping her on the shoulder and yanking the rope hard. Their posture and gestures were as strict and pure as kabuki poses.

Watching her performance from the wings I vacillated between thinking that it was far too soon for her to retire, and thinking that retiring at the height of her popularity with so many fans begging her to stay was actually the best way to bow out. Her hair was in pathetic disarray, and snow clung to her ruined under-kimono. Naomi closed her eyes in resignation as she staggered barefoot into the courtyard for punishment. Her strangely beautiful expressions and her pitifully crumbling posture were exquisite. As I watched her walk towards her awaiting punishment, growing desperate at the crescendo of the shamisen as she looked back towards her love, I found myself suddenly aware of the ephemeral beauty of a woman's body.

Naomi led Kusunose and me out of Club Otani and brought us to Dorobushi, a high-end restaurant. The restaurant's focus is on healthy cuisine with an emphasis on vegetable fare. It was different, but the special house sake was excellent.

Naomi's final film and farewell performance took place in 1979, almost twenty years earlier. And yet you would never know from looking at her that so much time had passed. Seeing her still radiant beauty made me feel like her farewell show had happened just yesterday.

We got fairly tipsy and ended up talking about the old days. Whether or not they were good days or not is debatable, but we couldn't help but feel nostalgic. Kusunose ended up tossing aside his notebook and just listened to us talk. Naomi had shifted her focus and worked hard to become a successful businesswoman, so it was likely that her judgment of the past wasn't entirely accurate anyway. To me, the memories of events twenty years ago were sweet and made me a little melancholic, but that was because I was in my sixties and given to sentimental nostalgia. Naomi hadn't the slightest hint of sentimentality about her past. We spent most of the conversation talking about Kiyoshi Atsumi who had passed away that same year. When Naomi finally broke up with Yamaoka she called Kiyoshi. "Oh, you broke up with him?" he asked. "Well, you're a very tough girl, Naomi. I'm sure you'll be just fine," he said, cheering her up.

Kiyoshi was very kind even to chorus girls and lowly porn actresses, she said, swallowing back tears as she talked about their friendship. Even though I was directly involved at the time I couldn't say much in response.

She had spoken with Kiyoshi before he died. "Yamaoka's doing great, he just had his sixty-third birthday. How's Terumi? Oh, so it's true that they split up? How is the child doing, I wonder?"

Women are far stronger than men when it comes to surveying the past in a cool, reserved way. Naomi wasn't like that in her youth, though. When she thought she was about to be dumped she'd call me in hysterics; when she found out her beloved assistant was sleeping with her boyfriend behind her back she'd lose her temper and slap her across the face. She was queen of the mood swing.

"Mr. Obayashi and I are bound by pure love," she had said, turning to me with a sickly sweet and utterly maddening smile. But just a few years ago she had divorced the same Mr. Obayashi, and was now single.

After her divorce Naomi was very depressed. She wrote me a long letter explaining what had happened. Just as with Yamaoka, Mr. Obayashi had cheated on her. After getting married Obayashi started up a karaoke school in Kumamoto, and Naomi had gone to great lengths helping him find people who wanted to enroll in classes. I was surprised when I received a karaoke school application form in the mail. I couldn't go all the way to Kumamoto to take classes, so I sent them a card congratulating them on the opening of the school. But the school didn't take off, and they had to shut down the business. In order to pay the bills Naomi did various jobs, going around town selling medical supplies, establishing a theatre troupe that performed at old folks' homes. The stories of her struggles during that time could fill a book. Eventually Naomi opened a club of her own. Just weeks after she opened shop and was seeing the beginnings of success, she was hit by a motorcycle which sent her flying thirty feet. She was hospitalized for a long time, during which her husband placed his priorities on pleasuring himself. Naomi found out about his adultery and became neurotic and depressed. Just like in her younger days, her fate was constantly zig-zagging up and down. After thinking things through she demanded a divorce, but her husband refused. They ended up taking their battle to court. It took a year before a settlement was reached.

In her letter Naomi didn't write anything ill of her ex-husband. Just as in her break-up with Yamaoka she blamed herself, saying she was the reason men turned evil during their relationships. Yamaoka was jealous of all the attention Naomi received as a result of her success as the Queen of Nikkatsu Roman Porno's S&M films, so he took out his frustration in the bed of another woman. Similarly Obayashi got jealous of how successful Naomi was at anything she tried her hand at; plus he must have envied the kind treatment she lavished on the customers of her club.

"So that's why I've made a resolution to never be with a man again. I would just feel sorry for anyone I was with. I'm better off alone. I'm much happier this way," she said earnestly.

We left Dorobushi and wandered through the bustling Hanabata district. We went into a pub that was famous for serving extremely fresh sashimi (from fish that was living right up until it was cut into sashimi). After polishing off a few rounds of sake, Naomi got pretty drunk.

"Can you really live the rest of your life single?" I asked, slurring my speech a little. "I mean, you've always been boy-crazy." I was just teasing her, but I instantly felt like I had said too much.

It seemed like Naomi was the type to go crazy over a guy, but in fact she didn't fall for just anyone. She was actually fairly reserved with her feelings, but once she fell for someone she fell hard. She'd become so attached that she'd be totally at the beck and call of whomever she was with. Because she was so attached to her man it would seem like she was crazy for the boys, but she hadn't fallen for anyone but Yamaoka and Obayashi. When some random guy fell for her and tried to hit on her, she'd turn such venom on him that I'd blush with embarrassment for the guy. It was that brand of street smarts and unyielding spirit that impressed me so much.

When she first found out about Yamaoka and Obayashi's infidelities, she confronted them on the verge of tears, but both of the men slyly explained away the evidence and brought her back down from the brink of hysterics. If someone told her she was simple, lacking in common sense and knowledge, she'd just shrug it off and laugh, saying that she could take compliments as well as criticism. Even though she was called the Queen of Nikkatsu Roman Porno she never let it get to her head.

She was always open and frank with everyone, and never once put on airs. I liked that part of Naomi best.

After Naomi retired, one of the producers from Nikkatsu, Mr. Okamura, came to discuss the future of the S&M film division with me. I had wanted to shut down the division after Naomi left, but Okamura wanted to continue production. Apparently Naomi made S&M so popular that it was too profitable to shut down. Both Mr. Okamura and another producer, Mr. Yuuki, finally talked me into continuing the division. We crowned successive queens of S&M—Junko Mabuki, Izumi Shima and Miki Takakura—all of whom had a soft spot for the male members of the crew; even I was showered with affection. But I respected Naomi most of all, simply because she remained a porn star until the end of her career. Several TV directors asked her to appear in a guest star role on their shows, but every time she would turn them down without hesitation, explaining, "I'm a porn actress."

In reality, she was afraid of working in a strange studio with a crew she didn't know. This reasoning might have been based on the same logic she used to argue against putting her money in a bank account, since she didn't know anyone at the bank, either.

The second, third and fourth queens of S&M secretly wanted a chance to work in films and TV shows outside the porn industry. They all had an inferiority complex that lurked just beneath the surface, and they were always sensitive about their status as second-rate actresses. Naomi, however, was different. She was a porn star, and that was all she ever wanted to be.

Naomi turned an intoxicated gaze to me. "I've totally cut myself off from men. Do you want to see the proof?" she asked saucily. "I put a magic spell on my body to keep men away."

"Let's see it then, you tease," I said, grinning. Naomi glanced towards Kusunose, who was half asleep and slumped over his drink.

"On second thought, maybe I shouldn't," she demurred, laughing shyly.

The pub was empty except for the three of us.

"It's fine. Show me!" "No, I'm too embarrassed." The two of us went on like this for a few minutes, and Kusunose finally caught on and suddenly stood and excused himself to go buy a pack of cigarettes.

Once he was gone Naomi led me by the hand to a table towards the back of the pub.

"I know you're going to think this is stupid. I haven't shown anyone this yet, so it's our little secret," she said, turning her back to me. "Pull down the back of my collar a bit, and you'll see it."

I pulled down the collar and admired the porcelain smooth sensuality of the nape of her neck. As I looked down further, I suddenly stopped and said, "Oh!"

"We used to sing this song a long time ago," Naomi said, and slowly swayed her body back and forth as she sang, in a soft alto voice, "Lady Yakuza: Red Peony Gambler."

Gamble away the bloom of your youth
Bluff with your body
Red Peony on fire

"Stupid," I tisked, and pulled my hand away suddenly as if her collar had burned me.

All across the milk white silky smooth expanse of her back was a tattoo of brilliant Hizakura cherry blossoms.

She laughed, somewhat self-deprecatingly, as she fixed her collar and turned to face me.

"During the yearlong divorce trial I got so angry that men could be so stubborn and stingy. I was so pissed I decided to cover my back with bright pink cherry blossoms. I felt renewed after I did it. I let my ex have the house, the land, everything. The only thing I still own is that little club. That's why I still work so hard to keep it going," she said.

In her final film for Nikkatsu, *Rope and Skin*, Naomi played Okoma Hizakura, a female yakuza. We had a fake tattoo of brilliant Hizakura cherry blossoms painted onto her soft, smooth skin. Seeing Naomi's real tattoo suddenly made me flash back to that film, the daring Okoma charging into the yakuza's hangout.

I don't know whether it was foolish or wise of Naomi to get a real tattoo. But such a tattoo made it painfully clear that she didn't want another man to get close to her ever again. She was completely dedicated to her new career as a businesswoman.

One of the managers at Club Otani kept calling the pub, asking Naomi to come back. The club was getting crowded, and the hostesses were worried that the madam wasn't around.

"Let's go back to the club and sing karaoke," Naomi said once Kusunose had returned. Naomi took my hand as we left the pub, and I couldn't help but say "stupid" again.

"But I've always been stupid," she laughed.

Club Otani was packed. As soon as we entered everyone cheered for Naomi and asked her to sing.

"Okay then, I'll sing an old enka song," she said and started singing Junko Fuji's "Lady Yakuza."

I am a proud yakuza gambler, but still a woman.
My long hair is wet, the Red Peony falters.
A woman's, a woman's regret—
As the night wears on the stars fall from the sky.

I've grown old, I thought to myself. Here I am, wishing I could shut my eyes to the present and go back twenty years to those good old days. An old man's sentimental longing, nothing more, nothing less. But as Naomi sang "Lady Yakuza," I couldn't help but think back to her performances in *Rope and Skin* and *O-Ryu's Passion*, the image of her tattoo-covered milk white skin flashing before my eyes. I was hopelessly nostalgic for the past. Led by Naomi's voice I staggered slowly towards her. I squinted back tears of melancholy as I stood and sang by her side.

ALSO FROM VERTICAL

Lala Pipo
by Hideo Okuda

"This sleazy novel is not recommendable for ladies or gentlemen." So reads the jacket of the Japanese edition of this collection of six dark, interrelated, tragicomic chapters dealing with themes of desire, inadequacy, and failure. As misheard by one of the characters, "a lot of people," is "Lala Pipo." $14.95/$16.95

"These human monsters, it turns out, could be as American as you or I, and their secret lives look distressingly familiar. Okuda successfully taps into the creep inside us all." *—The Stranger* (Seattle)

Innocent World
by Ami Sakurai

Enter a world of nihilism and self-destruction. Enter a world of rape, incest, and trauma. Enter a world of violence, drugs, and prostitution. Enter an innocent world.

Ami believes in nothing, hopes for nothing, and turns tricks because it's something to do. Her journey from the pit of despair to the precarious edge of something else captures the part of being seventeen that rarely makes it into words. A razor-sharp novella whose sheer intensity elevates misanthropy to the level of art. $11.95/$16.95

WWW.VERTICAL-INC.COM

Translucent Tree
by Nobuko Takagi

Chigiri, a divorced single mother, lives in the countryside town where she grew up, and her life seems to be going nowhere. When a documentary filmmaker revisits the town after thirty years, Chigiri, who was still a high school student back then, begins to feel like one again. Yet feelings aren't where it ends when a half-serious offer of prostitution is floated between the financially desperate Chigiri and Go, the visitor, who has since become successful in Tokyo. $19.95/$22.95

Outlet
by Randy Taguchi

Where would a shaman fit into modern society? Are trance states to be dismissed simply as fits of madness? Is the buffoonery of psychic hotlines all that the modern world has left of spiritual intuition? *Outlet* is a sexy psychological detective story that seeks to answer these questions. $15.95/$20.95

"Outlet is a sexually charged and intriguing New Age mystery that is smart and well-paced." —*Library Journal*

**Available wherever books are sold
and online at www.randomhouse.com**

WWW.VERTICAL-INC.COM